His phone rang. It was Alexa. His gut knotted. Why was she calling? Was something wrong? He punched the button to put the call on speaker.

"Alexa? What's wrong?"

"Gavin?" He winced at the quaver in her voice. "I think someone was looking in my window."

"Get away from the windows! I'm two minutes away."

He flipped the switch to turn on his siren and set his lights flashing. The last mile and a half of the trip took forever. Finally, he arrived, pulling into the short driveway. As he hopped out of the car, the door opened.

"Go inside," he ordered. "I'm going to take a look around."

He waited until she had complied, then circled the house. There were indeed footsteps by her kitchen windows. The curtains were closed now. Had they been earlier? The prints in the snow circled the house. Whoever it had been, they'd been watching her for more than a few minutes.

The stalker was bold, that was for sure. And determined. There was one thing Jackson was absolutely sure of.

Alexa Grant was in grave danger.

Dana R. Lynn grew up in Illinois. She met a man at a wedding who she told her parents was her future husband. Nineteen months later, they were married. Today they live in rural Pennsylvania with their three children, two dogs, one cat, one rabbit, one horse and six chickens. In addition to writing, she works as an educational interpreter for the deaf and is active in several ministries in her church.

Books by Dana R. Lynn

Love Inspired Suspense

Amish Country Justice

Plain Target
Plain Retribution
Amish Christmas Abduction
Amish Country Ambush
Amish Christmas Emergency

Presumed Guilty
Interrupted Lullaby

Visit the Author Profile page at Harlequin.com.

AMISH
CHRISTMAS
EMERGENCY

DANA R. LYNN

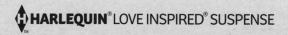

HARLEQUIN® LOVE INSPIRED® SUSPENSE

Recycling programs
for this product may
not exist in your area.

LOVE INSPIRED BOOKS

ISBN-13: 978-1-335-54410-0

Amish Christmas Emergency

www.Harlequin.com

Printed in U.S.A.

What shall we then say to these things?
If God be for us, who can be against us?
–Romans 8:31

For my nephew, Andrew David. We waited a long time for you, but you were worth the wait. Love you.

Acknowledgments

To my husband and children...you guys are my world. Love you.

Amy and Dee...I'd go crazy without you two and our monthly coffee hours.

Lee and Rachel...you have been a blessing to me in so many ways. Love you.

To my writer friends and critique partners...thanks for all your support and prayers through this journey.

To my Dream Team...I love you ladies! Your encouragement and support mean so much! My heart is so grateful!

To my editor, Elizabeth Mazer...thanks for all your wisdom and guidance.

To my agent, Tamela Hancock Murray...you are a powerhouse! Your faith and your drive inspire me.

Lord Jesus...I ask that my words and actions always bring You glory.

ONE

"Megan, has Noah Hostetler arrived yet?"

Concern bit at nurse practitioner Alexa Grant as she hovered by the receptionist's desk. It wasn't like Noah to be late. He was always at least half an hour early. She knew for a fact that when the Amish man hired a driver to take him to his medical appointments, he booked them with plenty of wiggle room. A quick glance outside made her grimace. When she'd driven to work that morning, it had been cold, but the sky had been clear. Now, three hours later, a heavy sheet of snow and ice pelted the glass windows of the small medical clinic.

It figured. Her lips twisted. There hadn't been any snow to speak of in LaMar Pond, Pennsylvania, back in November at Thanksgiving time. Now, only two weeks out from Christmas, the snow and freezing temperatures pounded the small town relentlessly, adding to the chaos of the season.

Chaos like the flu epidemic sweeping through northwestern Pennsylvania. It had hit LaMar Pond in the past three weeks. It was a virulent strain. One that was resistant to the vaccine. Several deaths had been reported throughout the affected area. It was hitting the local Amish community especially hard. In addition to her usual weekly home visits, Alexa had been out to see several children and one elderly woman already for the virus. Noah's family had been hit, as well. Thankfully, his wife and children were on the mend.

Megan, the pretty young receptionist, shook her head, never looking up from her computer. Alexa didn't take offense. Megan, like everyone else, was busier than usual. Even with the yearly shots, two nurses were already down with the flu. Nurses they couldn't afford to do without. This was a clinic funded chiefly by donations. There wasn't a hefty budget. The owners barely had enough staff to cover the clinic as it was.

The dispatch radio sent out a series of beeps. For a moment, the employees at the clinic paused, mostly out of habit, as many of the staff also worked shifts at the main hospital.

That particular beep pattern was for the ambulance service and volunteer fire department in the next town over. Any victims would be transported to the hospital. Static crackled briefly before it was replaced with the dispatcher's voice. Alexa winced. A four vehicle crash on the interstate. Conditions were bound to get worse. The weather forecast had said the snow was supposed to continue all day and into tomorrow.

Had Noah been in an accident, too? His usual driver was very cautious, but there were many other drivers out on the roads who were in too much of a hurry.

The dispatcher's voice stopped, and the cheery sounds of Christmas music filled the air. The dichotomy of danger and joy was jarring to her. No one else seemed bothered by it, though, so she put the thought aside.

Alexa glanced at the clock on the wall and felt her tension go up a notch. Noah was now ten minutes late. If he didn't show up in the next five minutes, the clinic's policy dictated that he would lose his appointment. That would keep the clinic from getting even further behind schedule. She gnawed on her bottom lip. It could also set Noah's recovery back a bit. Which would be a shame. Both his children were recovering from vicious cases of the flu, and he had come down with it, as well. Noah had chronically weak lungs, so he'd had a hard battle on his hands. But, hopefully, today's exam would show that he was truly on the mend.

If he showed up.

Needing something to do, she moved to the counter against the wall, took a mug off the shelf and made herself a cup of hot tea. Still, she couldn't get Noah out of her mind.

Alexa didn't get caught up in her patients' lives. She wouldn't allow herself that luxury. No, as a nurse practitioner, she learned the value of keeping a professional distance.

Actually, she tended to keep her emotional distance at all times, professional or not.

The one time she hadn't had nearly destroyed her.

She shook her head, refusing to give in to the memories that haunted her. Memories that had forced her to leave her home in Downers Grove, Illinois.

A tingle hit her between her shoulder blades. She hunched them slightly, suppressing a shiver. Nervously, she glanced toward the window again. No one was there. She couldn't quite shake the feeling that something was wrong. The feeling had dogged her all week. Like a dark cloud, always hovering over her head, blocking out the sun. At times, she'd have the sensation of being watched. Sometimes at work. Sometimes at home. Once when she was running errands in town. She'd made a valiant effort to remain positive, but it was starting to weigh on her.

Frustrated, she stirred her tea with more vigor than was called for. She so didn't need this stress. Hadn't she made the decision to move to this rural northwestern Pennsylvania town to heal from the tragedy that had devastated her and to rebuild her life? How was she to do that when she was always tense?

The sound of a rough engine outside the building caught her attention. Some of the tension drained out as she noticed Noah stepping out of the van. Finally. A sigh escaped her. Setting her tea mug down on a side counter, she scooped up Noah's file.

His driver started to drive off as Noah reached the clinic door. His hand was on the handle, and he started to pull the door open. A blast of cold air whooshed inside the busy waiting room, then the glass pane shattered with a loud crash. Everyone stilled, shocked. Noah stood with the door half open. A second gunshot blasted into the silence. Alexa screamed, dimly aware that others were screaming too as the young Amish man at the door swayed, a dark stain spreading across his shoulder. Not again. She wouldn't lose another patient.

In the midst of the madness, Alexa realized that the other patients were potential targets.

"Get down!" Running across the lobby, Alexa reached the door and grabbed on to Noah as he started to crumple to the ground. Yanking him inside the building, she yelled for help. One of the other employees appeared at her side. Together, they managed to pull Noah across the lobby and behind the receptionist's counter.

"Noah! Noah. Can you hear me?" No response. Leaning closer, she gently shook his shoulder. Her hand came away wet. A quick glance confirmed her fears. Her hand was covered with Noah's blood.

"An ambulance and the police are on their way." Megan fell to her knees beside Alexa, gauze bandages in her hands.

Alexa nodded her understanding. She grabbed the bandages and started to do what she could to stop the bleeding. Noah was still breathing, although there was a rasp to it she didn't care for. Whether that was from the virus or from the injury, she couldn't tell.

"Where's the doctor? Grab me a blanket, will you?"

Megan quickly left, returning in seconds with an armful of blankets.

"I haven't seen the doctor for almost an hour. He was in the back, treating patients. I'm amazed he didn't hear the commotion."

Alexa nodded to let Megan know she heard her. They needed to keep Noah warm. She was worried he could go into shock. "Cover him. I can't relieve the pressure on his wound."

On the floor, Noah moaned; his eyes were shut. Alexa encouraged him, keeping her voice calm, not letting on that inside she was a quivering mess.

"Come on, Noah. Fight this. You have a family to take care of," Alexa told her patient.

What was that? She straightened, closing her eyes to hear better. Yes! Sirens.

"Do you hear that, Noah? Sirens. The ambulance is on its way."

The next few minutes were frenzied. The ambulance crew arrived in a flurry of activity. Alexa sat back on her heels, letting the paramedics take over for her. She remained alert, ready to help in an instant if they called on her. She'd do whatever they needed to help Noah.

Another siren split the air. Red and blue strobe lights flickered on the walls, glinting off the shards of glass still on the floor. She shivered. She hadn't realized until now how cold the clinic had become with the door's window broken. But she could see little puffs emerging from people's mouths as they breathed.

A LaMar Pond police officer entered the building. He quietly began to talk with the staff and patients. As he worked the room, a second officer arrived. He sauntered in casually, but his bright blue eyes were anything but causal as they canvassed the room. His black hair was dotted with snowflakes, which melted as she watched.

"Parker, what do ya know?" he asked the other officer, his eyes still moving.

"Hey, Jackson," the first officer, Parker, responded. "The witnesses I've talked to so far said that the victim was entering the clinic when the window was shot out. There was another shot, and he was hit."

The second officer, Jackson, stiffened. "A sniper! We need to have the area searched. Have there been any more shots since the victim went down?"

She had been listening as Parker brought him up to speed on the situation. At this question, she spoke up. "I didn't hear any."

Both officers looked her way. "Nurse, we need to talk with everyone and get the area checked out. Then we'll be back to talk with you."

She nodded. They started to walk away. "Wait! The man who was shot…do you know how he is?"

"Unknown at this point," Parker said kindly.

Alexa frowned as a thought occurred to her. Someone needed to let Noah's family know what had happened. His wife should be by his side at a time like this. She bit her lip. She couldn't call her. The Hostetlers were Amish. The Amish didn't use modern technology, including telephones, inside their homes. As soon as the officers came back, she'd mention it.

Her attention was drawn back to the room as the officers began questioning the witnesses. More police arrived. Officer Jackson directed them to start a sweep of the rooftops and surrounding area, searching for their sniper. They briskly set about following his orders. Then he headed her way.

A shiver worked its way down her spine.

Small towns were supposed to be safe. LaMar Pond was proving to be the exact opposite. Her glance flickered toward the broken window. Once again, her peace had been shattered, just like the glass. In her mind, the image of the Noah being shot replayed in her mind like a horror movie. She would remember that sight for the rest of her life.

Who would commit such a crime?

Sergeant Gavin Jackson shook his head as he surveyed the damage. What a mess. A crew had arrived to clean up the broken glass in the entranceway. The crime scene had been hopelessly compromised, but that couldn't have been helped. Not with a waiting room full of patients. Plus, the injured man had been dragged through the scene, leaving a trail of melted snow, glass and blood.

It had saved his life, so it was worth it.

Gavin made his way across the room to the nurse practitioner. Her name was Miss Alexa Grant, the janitor he'd just interviewed had said. She was watching him, her blue-gray eyes wide and uncertain. Her blond hair was pulled back into a clip, revealing high cheekbones and a perfect oval face. She was probably the prettiest woman he'd seen in a long time.

What was he doing? He was here on police business. There was no reason for him to be noticing if she was pretty or not. Besides, pretty on the outside meant nothing. He knew that too well. And nothing would tempt him to get caught in the emotional trap of romance.

Not again. The price was too high to pay. His goal here was to find a sniper and protect these civilians. That's what he'd do.

"Miss Grant," he said, halting before her. "I'm Sergeant Jackson with the LaMar Pond PD. I would like to talk with you about what happened here this afternoon. I understand that you helped move the victim."

A slight shudder shook her slender frame, but her eyes never wavered. She had courage. He admired courage.

"Noah Hostetler is a patient here. He had an appointment, but he was late. He's never late." She hurried on, a concerned wrinkle forming on her brow. "Please, Sergeant Jackson. Noah has a wife. Naomi. And children. She won't know what's happened."

"I'll make sure she's notified, ASAP." Gavin shifted the clipboard he was holding. With his thumb, he clicked the pen in his hand several times. He hated standing still. "His driver said the van had slid off the road. They needed to be pulled out of the ditch, which got them running late."

"I wondered," she whispered. "If he'd been here on time, he would have been fine."

"You can't know that," Gavin said, even though he thought she was right. It did no good to dwell on what might have happened. It couldn't be changed. No matter how much he wished it could.

Alexa sighed. It was a small sound, but it contained a wealth of hurt and confusion. "I just don't understand why anyone would shoot at him. He's a young father. A husband. His wife makes the best cookies."

He blinked at the last comment. "It is possible that the shooter wasn't specifically targeting Mr. Hostetler. It could have been random. Maybe someone had a grudge against the clinic. It's fairly new, right?"

"Yes." She drew out the word slowly. "I have only been here for a few months. But it was opened within the past two years. The doctor who started it wanted a clinic that those who lived too far from the hospital and those in the Amish community could visit."

Gavin talked with the pretty nurse for another few moments before moving on. No one seemed to have noticed anything. The doctor on call had been in the back room doing his dictation. Two of the nurses were out sick. The patients were a mixture of townspeople and Amish, mostly elderly or children with their mothers.

"Jackson!"

Hearing his name called, he turned and moved to where Parker was motioning to him. "What's up?"

Sergeant Ryan Parker smiled, a slight lifting of the right corner of his mouth. Gavin knew his buddy well enough to know that the smile was practically an announcement that he'd found something important.

"I just got off the phone with the hospital. The man who was shot?" Gavin motioned for him to continue. "Well, he said something in the ambulance about catching a brief glance of a man with a gun as he was falling. Not a clear glance, mind you. But maybe we'll be able to glean enough from his statement to get a real lead."

That sounded promising. He wasn't going to get his hopes up, though. If the man hadn't gotten a good look, well, it might not help at all. It wasn't as if a man would stand out carrying a gun during hunting season in Pennsylvania.

"How's he doing? Our victim?"

Parker shrugged. "I'm not sure. He was being prepped for surgery. The person I talked with did feel that it was a good sign that he was conscious and thinking clearly. His wife has been contacted and is being brought to the hospital. We should know more later on today."

"Did you get the scene on your body cam?"

Parker gave him a thumbs-up. "Done. I already sent it to the station. We can go through it there. See if anything stands out."

"Okay. I guess we're done here then. Meet you back at the station."

Parker smiled and departed. Gavin zipped up his coat. He hesitated before leaving. Surely that nurse, Miss Grant, would appreciate hearing that her patient was still alive. Before he could talk himself out of it, he walked over to her. She was talking to the men who were covering the broken window with plastic. When she saw him, she halted her conversation and moved away from them.

"Sergeant?"

"Jackson. Or Gavin." Now why had he said that? It wasn't like they needed to be on a first-name basis. And besides, very few people called him Gavin. Okay, make that three people called him Gavin. His mom, dad and his brother.

But Gavin hadn't talked to his brother since Sam had betrayed him in the worst possible way.

Get it together, Jackson. He'd promised himself after Sam and Lacey's betrayal that he'd never let himself be humiliated that way again. His parents were concerned that he'd wind up alone. Well, maybe he'd be alone, but at least he'd know that he was living his life on his terms. That no one was taking advantage of him.

So why was he inviting a complete stranger to call him by his first name? He'd always hated his name.

She smiled briefly. It was a very tired smile. "Gavin, then. I'm Alexa."

He changed his mind. He liked the way his name sounded when she said it. He really needed to focus.

Touching her lightly on the elbow, he pointed to an area away from the others in the room. Alexa seemed to understand. She led him behind the receptionist's counter. Turning to face him, she raised an eyebrow and waited.

"I know you were worried about Noah

Hostetler. I wanted to let you know that he made it to the hospital. He's going into surgery, but he was conscious and alert. His wife is on the way to join him."

"Oh!" Her blue-gray eyes glittered with unshed tears. "Thank you so much for letting me know. I was worried about him."

He reached out and patted her shoulder. It was an awkward movement. Her eyes widened, and she jerked back slightly, flushed. He dropped his arm instantly, feeling like an idiot. What was he thinking? He had never been the touchy-feely type. It just wasn't his style. He'd blame it on exhaustion. His shift was supposed to have ended two hours ago, but between the accident and now this shooting, he would be on the job for at least two more hours before he could head home and sleep.

"Hey, Alexa, what is this? It looks like you had a delivery," the receptionist said.

Something flashed in her eyes before she averted them. Was it embarrassment? Fear? Whatever it was, she didn't look happy to be receiving a delivery. In fact, she looked downright annoyed about it. She looked at the box the receptionist, Megan, pointed to with a scowl. Something was going on here. Although, it really was none of his business. The flowers were probably from an ex. He glanced at her left hand. No rings. Not even an indentation. So she probably wasn't married or recently divorced.

"When did that get here?"

"I don't know. I just saw it sitting here."

"Miss Grant!" A man in a doctor's coat strode up to them, scowling. "Haven't I asked you not to get your deliveries here? This is a medical facility!"

"Yes, Dr. Quinton. I'm sorry, but I have no idea who's sending them."

Well, that was interesting.

The doctor wasn't appeased. "Tell the florist to stop making deliveries here then."

"Yes, Dr. Quinton. I told the florist that. Last week. This is from a different florist. One from out of town."

The man huffed. "See that it doesn't happen again." He turned abruptly and left. Alexa tossed the narrow box on the counter. It bounced, and the lid fell off. A single red rose dropped onto the countertop. A note was in the box. She picked it up. The color drained from Alexa's face. Concerned, Gavin stepped forward and grabbed the note from her shaking hand.

"It's your fault he's dead. You're mine. Don't forget it again."

TWO

Alexa accepted the bottled water that Gavin brought to her with a smile of gratitude. She needed to have something in her hands to keep them from fidgeting. She sat in the conference room at the LaMar Pond Police Department. Sergeant Parker seated himself in a chair on the other side of the table. Gavin stood right inside the door. The rose and the note she'd received had been whisked away into evidence. She didn't complain. If she never saw another rose again, that would be great. She never would have guessed that her day would have turned out this way.

Unscrewing the cap, she lifted the bottle to her lips and took a long drink. She hadn't realized how thirsty she was. How long had it been since she had last eaten? Too long. She had not had a chance to grab her lunch, and then things had gotten crazy. She needed something soon if she didn't want her blood sugar levels to crash. She wasn't feeling dizzy or confused yet, although she was a bit shaky. That could be from the shock of the morning's events, though. But what if it wasn't? She wasn't fatigued, though, which was a good sign. She had her sugar tablets in her bag, but she should eat something too.

"Do you need anything else? Something to eat?" Gavin inquired.

She smiled at him, relieved. "If it wouldn't be too much trouble. I was really sick years ago and developed type two diabetes. I'm feeling a little shaky. It's probably nothing, but I don't want to take the chance."

Gavin's eyes widened with alarm. "You have diabetes? Hang on!" He bolted out the door. She stared at the empty doorway, mouth open. She hadn't expected him to react like that. A chuckle from Sergeant Parker drew her attention back to the room. He shrugged when she lifted her eyebrows at him. Well, she might as well make use of the time. Opening her purse, she found her testing kit and quickly pricked her finger to test her levels. She grimaced at the number on the small screen. Definitely too low. Hopefully, Gavin would bring her something she could use. A few minutes later, Gavin returned. He had a tray in his hands. "I went to the cafeteria and found some orange juice for you." He took it off the tray and handed her the carton.

Gratefully, she accepted the juice and opened it. The juice was sweet and cold. Finishing it off, she tossed the empty carton in the garbage can.

Gavin tossed to the remaining items on the tray. "I also got some food for you, seeing as you missed lunch. Eat what you want. Don't worry about whatever is left." He noticed her kit and nodded. "Good. I see you've already tested."

She examined the food he'd brought, pleasantly surprised. This was a man who knew diabetes. Salad, some sort of plain lean meat—turkey or chicken, she couldn't tell which—and a small cup of applesauce. Her nutritionist had told her to limit her carbs, but make sure her meals were centered around protein and veggies. Interesting. Judging by his reaction, he'd dealt with someone with type two diabetes before.

"Do you need anything else?" He hovered near her. If she said she did need something else, he'd probably run out the door again to get it. She quickly tried to put him at ease.

"No, thank you, Gavin. I'm good." She flashed a smile his way before picking up a bite of the meat. Chicken. She was being fanciful, but she could practically feel her blood sugar level stabilizing again as she chewed.

Nodding, Gavin proceeded to close the door. It was time to get down to business.

Sergeant Parker threw Gavin a look that could only be described as surprised. Why? Because she addressed the other cop by his first name? Was that wrong? He told her to. She decided that whatever it was, it wasn't important.

A laugh trickled out of her. It was a laugh filled with stress and nerves and very little humor. "I feel like I'm in trouble here."

"Nah." Gavin shrugged. "We just need to figure out what we're dealing with to keep you and everyone involved safe."

Peeking up under her lashes, she watched as Gavin stalked around the table to sit across from her. He was not a man who liked to sit; she could see that immediately. Even though his pose was casual—leaning back against the chair, long legs stretched out under the table so that his feet popped out next to hers—she could see the tension that danced across his broad shoulders. He had a careful smile on his face, but his jaw was rigid.

No, Gavin Jackson was a man who liked to move.

Not that she could blame him. She'd prefer to be almost anywhere than sitting in a police station right now, no matter how gorgeous the sergeants were.

Heat crept up her face at the thought. Great. Did they notice? Sergeant Parker was writing something on a tablet. Good. And Gavin…was staring right at her, head tilted, a half grin on his face. Wonderful. Well, she certainly wasn't going to tell him she'd been thinking about him. Hopefully, he wouldn't ask.

He shrugged and sat up a bit straighter, pulling his legs back to his side of the table.

"One thing about all this that might be to our advantage is that our sniper obviously thinks Mr. Hostetler is dead."

"That's a good thing?" she blurted.

"Absolutely," Parker answered. "If he thinks his target is dead, then Hostetler is easier to protect."

She nodded slowly. She could see that. If her admirer—she shuddered—thought that Noah was dead, he wouldn't go after him again.

"Alexa." She raised her gaze to Gavin's face.

The smile was gone. "How long have you been getting flowers from someone?"

How long had it been? She bit her lip as she considered. "I moved here in August. So I guess they started late October. Not frequently. The first time I received a rose, I thought Megan had brought it in to spruce up the receptionist's counter. There wasn't a note or anything. It sat there for a day before she asked if I wanted my flower. They've been coming every two weeks. At first I thought the whole secret admirer thing was really corny." She took a sip of water, giving herself time to organize her thoughts.

Gavin shifted in his seat. "You looked irritated when the delivery came. Was there something about the flowers that made you uncomfortable or nervous?"

"Nervous? Yeah. I was afraid my boss would fire me. He'd been okay the first time. But as they kept coming, he grew angrier with each delivery. I don't know why it bothered him so much, but I called the florist that had been used for the last delivery and told them not to accept any more for that address."

"Were all the flowers from florists?"

Shaking her head, she answered, "No. It was about half and half. I'm not sure how the others were delivered. I would come to work and find them."

Sergeant Parker was typing on a laptop. She couldn't tell if he was paying attention or not.

A moment later, she got her answer. "Well, this last one wasn't from a florist, either," he said.

"The name on the box," she began.

Gavin looked over at the laptop. "That name on the box is for a florist in Chicago. No way the flower was from there."

She cocked her head at him. "Why not? I've received flowers from there several times. Plus I used to live near Chicago. When my fiancé died fifteen months ago, I remember seeing flowers from Bressler's at the funeral home."

She definitely did not like the look on Gavin's face.

Shaking his head, Gavin turned the laptop so it was facing her. The image on the screen was a building that had been decimated by a fire. A hollow sensation blossomed in the pit of her stomach. The headline read, Bressler Family Florist Destroyed by Arson.

"The place was never rebuilt," Gavin informed her.

It felt as if the air had been sucked from the room. "When?" she managed to gasp out.

"Does the article say when the shop burned down?" She ignored the sympathy on his face. She didn't need sympathy. She needed answers.

"Yeah," he answered after scouring the article again. "It burned down three years ago. The arsonist was never caught. The owners had an apartment right above the store. It was destroyed also. Three bodies were found when the fire was investigated. The owners and their son had apparently all perished in their sleep."

She slumped. The flowers she'd received had been after the florist shop was long gone. She'd never checked. Another thought struck. "What does it mean that there were flowers from that place at Brett's funeral?"

"It means you might have a stalker. It also means that your stalker may have been the same person who burned down the building. At the very least, we know he had access to the building."

Setting the bottled water on the table, she covered her face with her hands. Suddenly, she was so tired. Lethargy seeped into her skin and worked its way down her body. A shiver caught her by surprise. It was difficult to tell if she was shivering because it was cold or if it was a delayed reaction to the horrific events of the past few hours.

"Hey, Alexa." Gavin's voice brought her back to the present. "We will find whoever this nutcase is. You know that, right? We will do everything we can to protect you."

She nodded, more to make him feel better than because she believed him. After all, how would they find someone if they had no idea who the person could be? Or why the person was fixated on her.

Sergeant Parker closed his laptop. "Do you have any thoughts about who could be stalking you?"

She racked her brain to come up with possible suspects, but no one came to mind. "No, sorry. I can't think of anyone. I want to go home."

All she wanted to do was to go home, lock the doors and the windows, and snuggle with her cat on the couch. Maybe she'd even call her brother, Allen. Although he'd no doubt ask her what was bothering her, as she never called him when something wasn't wrong. Her brother loved her, but he was so much older than her and lived so far away that he didn't give her too much thought. She received a Christmas card every year from his wife and a phone call on her birthday. He'd never even seen her apartment. No. She'd be better off dealing with this alone.

"Soon," Gavin promised. "Let's finish here, then I'll let you go."

She nodded. If it would help catch whoever hurt Noah, she'd do whatever the police said.

Gavin hesitated. "Alexa, we need to know what happened to Brett. How did your fiancé die?"

She'd known it was coming. And she'd thought she was prepared for the question. But the way the question came at her, forcing her to put the two situations together, chilled her blood. Were they connected?

The sudden conviction that they *were* connected caused her to blurt out, "I think he was murdered."

Gavin and Parker exchanged a glance. "You *think* he was murdered?" Gavin asked.

A grimace twisted her face. Then it smoothed into resignation. "I do now. At the time it never occurred to me. It wasn't something we were looking at. And, honestly, it just never would have occurred to me."

"Okay, Alexa. Why not start back at the beginning? What happened with your fiancé?"

Her head dropped for a moment. He could

almost see her trying to collect her thoughts and gather her courage. Admiration flickered briefly before he squashed it. Leaning forward, he waited.

"Brett Stevens and I had been dating for six months." His heart wrenched at the sorrow on her face, in her voice. "We had gone to high school together, but never really knew each other. There were over five hundred students in our graduating class. We met up again at a five-year get-together and just clicked. We dated for six months before we got engaged. I know that doesn't seem like a long time, but we'd been talking marriage since the second month. We'd gotten engaged just five days before he died. I was over the moon."

She swallowed. He knew that she was struggling, but to her credit, she kept going. "I went to a conference, and when I came home, he was in the hospital. An overdose. No one even knew we were engaged. Brett wanted to wait to announce it."

The heartache in her eyes was painful to even watch. But he made himself. Maybe if he could get some answers for her, she'd have some peace.

"So he was in the hospital…" he said when the silence grew too long.

She ran a hand through her shoulder-length blond hair. "Yeah. He was actually supposed to be one of my patients. Isn't that ironic?" She huffed a bitter laugh. "When I told the head nurse who he was, she put another nurse in charge of his case. During the night shift, he was somehow given the wrong IV. He went into cardiac arrest. They were unable to revive him."

She stood, began to pace. "I was investigated because I was on duty that night. All the night staff were, but the police looked especially hard at me because of our relationship. Something about the significant other often being the culprit. To make matters worse, I had gone in to visit him during my break." Alexa shook her head. "It was like being on one of those TV crime shows."

No doubt. "I'm guessing that you were cleared of any wrongdoing." It wasn't really a question. If she hadn't been, she would never have been hired as a nurse practitioner again.

"Yes. By the police. But the other nurses at the hospital were noticeably colder to me. I could tell that they weren't convinced. Someone started the rumor that I had driven him to attempt to kill himself and then had finished the job. It was horrible. I knew that wasn't the case, but still, I did wonder if it was my fault. If I had failed him. The guilt nearly destroyed me. Which is why I handed in my notice and sought out a new home in a quiet town where nothing exciting ever happened."

"Why do you think you failed him?"

The glance she flung in his direction clearly said she thought he was being thick. "Seriously? I'm a nurse. I came back from a medical conference to find the man I planned to marry had been admitted into the hospital after supposedly trying to kill himself."

"Surely, though, you knew you weren't at fault when he died at the hospital."

Alexa shrugged. "I wasn't the nurse taking care of him, so obviously I knew that I hadn't made the mistake with the IV. However, I thought that if I had realized he'd been depressed and gotten him help, he wouldn't have been in the hospital to begin with."

"Alexa, I will look into his death and the situation at the hospital. I will say this—I find it too much of a coincidence that both your fiancé and a man under your care at a medical facility have been hurt, or worse. Add to the mix the flowers that you got from a flower shop destroyed by arson." He tightened his lips. He knew in his gut that Brett had been murdered.

Without absolute proof, though, he was reluctant to voice the thought. Even though he was sure both Parker and Alexa were thinking the same thing.

"Alexa? Are you all right? Maybe you should sit down." Parker's concerned voice broke into his thoughts.

Looking up at the woman standing on the other side of the table, he understood why. If he thought her face was white before, it was completely colorless now. For a second, he feared she'd faint. He stood and moved to her side. Gently he urged her back to her seat. When she sat, he pulled out the chair beside her and sank into it.

"Alexa?" He touched her shoulder.

Finally, she turned her head, slowly, like it took great effort. "He followed me, didn't he? The man stalking me followed me from Chicago. I hadn't realized that someone was watching me there, too."

That startled him. "Too? Alexa, has someone been watching you?"

The urgency of his voice seemed to jerk her out of her of the dark place she'd gone in her mind.

"I don't know. I can't be sure. It's just that

sometimes…sometimes I feel like someone's watching me. You know the feeling?"

Both sergeants nodded.

"Where are you when this happens?" Parker asked. "At work? Home?"

She raised her hands, palms up. "Yes, to both. Home, work, once outside the post office. I never actually saw anyone suspicious. Nor have I noticed the same person in several places."

Gavin digested that information, not liking it at all. "What about other incidents at the clinic? Anything unusual or suspicious stand out to you?"

When she shook his head, he held in a sigh. Not from impatience with her. She was a victim here. No, he was impatient with the idea that he had to let her go home without any assurance that the attacker was beyond bars. Who would protect her?

He would have to make sure that she was safe.

"Was it my fault?" she asked in a small, dull voice. "Did Brett die and did Noah get shot because of me?"

"No!" She flinched from the force of his response. He gentled his voice. "No. Alexa, it's not on you that some creep is following you.

You did not ask for it. And you certainly don't deserve it. No woman does."

"I get that, but Brett—"

He cut her off. "Brett loved you, right? I am sure that he wouldn't want you to blame yourself."

Gavin waited for her nod, then he stood. "Okay. Here's what we're going to do. I'll see about getting you some protection where you live. Obviously, you'll need to take some time off work—"

"I can't!" she interrupted him.

"What do you mean you can't?" Why would anyone want to go to work when someone was literally gunning for them?

Parker stood and came around the table. "Alexa, you're in danger. Going to work will bring that danger to the others who work there."

"Gah!" She exploded into a standing position so fast her wooden chair fell over with a loud clatter. Parker stooped to pick it up. Alexa strode to the window. The tension was vibrating off her. "I get what you're saying. I do. But I don't have a choice. Maybe if we weren't in the middle of a flu epidemic. As it is, the clinic is already short-staffed. We have patients who depend on us."

Gavin considered the situation. "Hold on for just a minute, okay?" He strode to the door.

"He's always on the go. Don't mind him," he heard Parker murmur to Alexa as he exited. He rolled his eyes, smiling briefly to himself. The amusement was short-lived.

He had a job to do. A woman to protect, and a stalker to find. A stalker who had already murdered in order to get close to his obsession.

A stalker who would kill again unless Gavin could stop him.

THREE

Using a knuckle, Gavin rapped sharply on Chief Paul Kennedy's office door. Impatiently he waited for the chief to answer. He was getting ready to knock again when Lieutenant Jace Tucker strolled past him.

"The chief's not in, Jackson," Tucker informed him. "He had to go with his wife to the doctor. He said he should be back in the next hour or so. Anything I can help you with?"

"Is Irene okay?" He hated to think of anything being wrong with the chief's feisty redhaired wife. Irene was well-loved by all the officers. Paul Kennedy was her second husband. Her first, Tony Martello, had been a solid cop. And a good friend. Four years ago, he'd been killed in the line of duty. The loss had been devastating to all involved. Especially to Irene. They were all happy when she and the chief had found each other.

She was also Lieutenant Tucker's sister. He didn't seem too worried. So it couldn't be that bad. Right?

"Nothing serious," Tucker said, confirming his thoughts. "What do you need?"

Switching gears, Gavin related what he'd learned so far. "What I'd really like to do is to order some sort of protection for Alexa."

At this moment nothing was more important than the frightened woman sitting in the conference room. "The woman ran from Chicago. And all evidence points to her stalker being from there, too."

Lieutenant Tucker straightened, his gaze sharpening. "Really? Let's put this on a priority level. I will inform the chief when he gets back. Can you hang with Miss Grant until we get the details worked out?"

He ignored the jolt of relief at the words. He should not, under any circumstances, have a preference for which officer stayed with Alexa. Nor should he be glad to have an excuse to stay with her.

The sooner he got her back to her place and another officer watching over her, the better. He'd been with her only a couple of hours and she was already messing with his mind. He didn't need that. Hadn't his dealings with

Lacey taught him anything? He was better off alone than setting himself up for that kind of heartbreak. And heartbreak and disappointment it would be. He was the kind of man that women liked until someone steady and smooth-talking came along. Someone like his brother, Sam.

He wasn't going there.

Alexa's life was in danger. He was chasing her stalker turned sniper. As far as he was concerned, that was as far as their connection would go. Could go. He refused to allow it to become anything more.

"I can do that, Lieutenant Tucker," he said. "What kind of plans are you thinking of?"

He didn't mean to be pushy, but he needed something concrete here.

Lieutenant Tucker gave him a level stare, and his right eyebrow twitched, but he didn't give Gavin any grief. Probably because Tucker himself had once had to protect a woman from a killer. A woman who was now Lieutenant Tucker's wife. *Irrelevant.* Shoving the annoying thought away, he focused once again on his superior officer. "I'm sure we could do some sort of drive-by. Like I said, I will run it by the chief when he gets back. We're limited on how much surveillance we can do. But we'll do our best."

"Yeah, that'll have to work." He ran a hand through his hair, thinking rapidly. "Here's what I'll do. I'll drive Alexa back to get her car. Then I'll follow her to her place and check it out. Maybe Parker can meet me there, and we can canvas the neighborhood, talk to the neighbors. See what's the situation there."

"Sounds good. I'll pass your message along to the chief when I see him."

There was nothing more to do at the station. He needed to confer with Parker. One of them needed to get to the hospital and get Noah Hostetler's statement the minute he was out of surgery and conscious. Amish folk didn't particularly go out of the way to converse with cops. However, given that he'd already told someone he had caught a glimpse of the sniper, Gavin didn't think the man would protest answering a few questions. Gavin retraced his steps back to where he'd left Alexa with Parker. They were talking quietly when he entered.

"Hey, Parker. One of us needs to go to the hospital." He didn't go into details. Parker was a smart man and an experienced officer. He'd be able to connect the dots. He switched his gaze to the anxious woman. The shadows drenching her eyes tugged at him, despite his desire to not be moved. It might take a while, but he would do everything in his power to clear away those shadows. "Alexa, how 'bout I drive you to get your car, and then we can head back to your house?"

She caught her lip between her teeth and blinked up at him. As her blue-gray eyes zeroed in on him, he knew that she wasn't going to agree with his plan. He waited for her argument.

Gavin fought against the frustration that was tearing at him. All he wanted was to find the stalker who was after her and give him a lengthy stay in a prison cell. Letting his emotions get out of hand would only get in his way. He couldn't afford that kind of complication. If he was to keep his wits about him and work with a clear mind, he needed to stay detached.

Especially from pretty blondes like the one gazing up at him. Nope. Not going there.

"Just say it, Alexa. Whatever's on your mind, just go ahead and say it."

She smiled slightly. "If you don't mind, I would like to go to the hospital with whoever is going. See how Noah is doing, and if his wife has arrived yet. I'll never be able to sleep until I know how they're coping."

He just wanted to get her home and locked up tight. The thought of her being out in the open when there was a sniper after her didn't sit well with him. Gearing up to tell her no, they couldn't visit the hospital, he glanced into those blue-gray eyes. The denial never made it past his lips.

After all, he had just said that they needed to go there. It might as well be him. Plus, Tucker did tell him to stick close until they had a plan approved.

"Sure. Parker, I'll take Alexa to the hospital. Cover the details there. We have to get her neighborhood checked out."

"I'll go ahead and start on that, Jackson."

He threw a grin toward Parker. "I was so hoping you'd say that, buddy."

"Yeah, I figured." Parker waved his hand at them in a shooing motion.

Alrighty, then. Alexa's stalker had already escalated to the point of violence. Violence that possibly had led to at least one death. If his suspicions proved to be true, then he was also responsible for the deaths when the florist shop had burnt down. It was only a matter of time before he struck out again.

Unless he could stop him.

Check out her neighborhood? Alexa paused, her coat halfway on. "Why do you have to check out my neighborhood? It's a very quiet one. Nothing ever happens there."

"Until we can narrow things down a bit, everyone around you is a potential suspect. I have requested some security for you. Lieutenant Tucker suggested that a police car do a periodic drive-by to keep an eye on your place. He's going to run that by the chief and let me know for sure. Hopefully, if someone is watching your home, that will keep them away. You have good locks on your place, right?" Gavin asked.

Irritation fled. A melting warmth took its place. It had been years since anyone worried over her well-being. She gave herself a mental shake. She wouldn't go all soft because someone asked her to lock her doors.

"I have locks." She hesitated. "Actually, they're kind of old locks. I don't think it would take too much for anyone to breach them."

Gavin and Sergeant Parker exchanged glances.

"What?" She heard the defensive tone in

her voice. "Until today, I had no idea I had a stalker. In the neighborhood where I live, half the people don't even bother locking their houses."

Their faces grew grimmer. "Well, you're going to lock yours," Gavin said.

Her shoulders stiffened, but she didn't argue. Independence was one thing, but arguing when she knew he was right wouldn't help the situation.

"Alexa." She turned her gaze to Sergeant Parker. "I'm also wondering if you would consider installing dead bolts on your doors."

"Of course," she responded quickly. "If it's that important, I will check on dead bolts tomorrow." Was it her imagination, or did some of the tension leave Gavin's shoulders when she agreed?

"We'll be by to check on your neighbors, make sure none of them are your admirer. Once we can rule them out, I'll feel a whole lot better about your being in your home by yourself."

Sergeant Parker nodded at Gavin's words.

She didn't like the sound of that at all. The idea that one of her neighbors might be her stalker had never crossed her mind. Briefly, she considered what she knew about the people who lived around her. Not much, she realized with some shame. Since leaving Chicago, she'd kept to herself. She had no real friends in the area. Sure, she got along with Megan, but they were colleagues. Megan had tried several times to convince her to go grab coffee or go to a movie with her. Each and every time, Alexa had shut her down with one excuse or another. Hence, here she was, in the police station, a stalker on her tail, and unable to account for her neighbors.

Suddenly, home had lost some of its appeal.

It is what it is. Deal with it. That was her lifelong motto. It held true in this instance, as well.

Gavin quirked one brow at her. "I'm fine," she said, tossing her blond hair over her shoulder. With more than a touch of defiance, truth be told. She would not let the man who was stalking her control her life. She might have to be careful, but that didn't mean that she had to completely give up her life. Such as it was. However, if someone was out to get her, her best way to protect her colleagues and neighbors was to avoid getting too close to them. Right?

Gavin started moving toward the door. She shook her head, willing herself to focus on the here and now, and followed him. When they arrived at his silver police car, he stepped in front of her to get the door. Whipping it open with an outrageous flourish, he bowed slightly. "Your carriage."

Oh, my. The handsome grin and roguish wink he tossed so casually toward her made her heart skip a beat. Sergeant Gavin Jackson was a charmer, that was for sure. Come to think of it, she remembered two of the nurses giggling about him a month or so ago. It seemed one of them had been at Sergeant Parker's engagement party. Gavin had flirted with the girl, but nothing ever came of it.

"You'd think a man that charming would have a date every night of the week," she recalled the nurse saying.

"Yeah, but the way I hear it, Sergeant Jackson doesn't date. Not ever."

Why? she wondered. What had happened to this handsome man that he had secluded himself?

Just like she had. She shook off the thought. Whatever his reason was, it was certainly none of her business. Of course, she could ask, but she'd never do that. Even if the curiosity was itching inside her mind.

"You gonna get in?" Gavin's voice snapped

her out of her thoughts. Blushing, she moved past him and folded herself into the seat. He shut the door gently and strode to his own side. When he got in the car, he glanced her way. "I didn't mean that to sound rude. Sorry. I have a habit of just blurting out what I think. Are you okay?"

Some of her embarrassment melted away at his sincere apology. The man was a chameleon, sometimes blunt, sometimes charming. But apparently he also had a noble spirit. How refreshing.

"I'm fine. Well, as fine as can be expected. I just realized that I never made the effort to get to know my neighbors. I'm disturbed at having so little idea about who lives near me."

"I wouldn't fret about it. It happens." He shrugged it off.

She rolled her eyes at his casual response.

The rest of the ride was silent. At the hospital, they were informed that Noah was out of surgery and in recovery. His wife had arrived and had been in to see him. Relieved, Alexa made for the elevator, aware of Gavin's steady tread behind her. There was something comforting in knowing that he stood at her back.

In the recovery area, Naomi Hostetler stood to greet them. "My Noah is going to be fine."

She smiled as she spoke, but the strain was visible in her eyes.

"I'm so glad, Naomi. What did the doctors tell you?" Alexa took the Amish woman's hands in her own.

"He said the surgery went *gut*. My husband will come home soon."

"Do you need anything in the meantime?"

The Amish woman shook her head. "*Nee. Denke.* We have a special fund for things like hospital visits and surgeries."

Alexa nodded, relieved. She had been concerned that this would be too much of a financial hardship for the family. She was more than willing to help out in any way that she could, but knew that her efforts wouldn't amount to much in the face of the medical bills that were sure come. Working in the field of medicine had given her a keen appreciation for how costs could stack up so quickly.

"Nurse Grant?"

Alexa turned to see the receptionist at the desk. Being a nurse practitioner, she sometimes was required to do shifts at the hospital, too. Which meant that she was known to most of the doctors and nurses on the staff.

"Yes?"

"There's a phone call for you." The woman

held out the phone to her. Without hesitation, Alexa stepped forward and took it from her outstretched hand.

"This is Nurse Grant. May I help you?"

"Don't let me down again, Alexa."

The phone went dead.

Alexa dropped the phone. It hit the floor with a sharp crack. The battery door flew off and the battery fell out.

"Alexa!" Gavin was beside her, holding on to her elbow. "Alexa, what is it?"

She lifted her face to his. She was shaking so hard, it was difficult to get the words out.

"It was him," she whispered. His face hardened. "He knew I was here."

Even now, he was watching her.

FOUR

Alexa watched Gavin and his colleagues as they investigated the phone call. They were thorough, she had to admit it. Everyone was questioned. The phone records were checked.

Still, she wasn't surprised when it came to nothing. The phone used to call her turned out to be a burner phone. No doubt one that was thrown out right after the call. At least that was Gavin's take on it. She hadn't known him long, but she trusted his instincts. Those related to his job, that was. He stood on the other side of the room, talking quietly on his phone to Sergeant Parker.

She wasn't alone, though. Naomi had joined her. Her husband was out of surgery, but he was still unconscious. She flicked her glance to Gavin again. The charming man who had ushered her into his vehicle earlier had vanished. In his place was the serious and dedicated sergeant she had first seen at the clinic this morning. It was comforting having him near.

The image of her brother's face entered her mind. He had no idea that his sister had been targeted by a stalker again.

Maybe I should call Allen. Let him know what's going on.

No, she rejected that thought again. Her brother would no doubt try to rearrange his schedule to come to be with her. And then he'd do his best to persuade her to quit her job and move in with him.

Like that would go over well. Alexa got along well with her sister-in-law. From a distance. But Melissa was just a little too high-maintenance for her comfort. She could still remember all the fuss and drama at her bridal shower years ago. It would probably be worse now that they had a new baby in the house.

Yeah, calling Allen wasn't something she planned on doing. Maybe once they caught this guy she'd take the vacation she'd been meaning to take and go visit them. A short visit.

If they caught the stalker.

She shuddered. Living under the weight of knowing someone was watching her would be unbearable.

"It will be fine." Naomi patted the back

of her fist lightly. She hadn't realized she'd clenched her hands. "Do you trust *Gott*?"

Did she trust God? Puzzled, she considered her companion. "I can't say that I've really thought about God," she admitted.

It's not that she didn't believe God existed. She'd just never had any use for Him in her life.

"Trust in God is a good thing."

She hadn't heard Gavin approach. Startled, she swiveled her neck to look up at him. He approached with a jaunty stride. His blue eyes cut in her direction, pinning her with his level stare. Not intimidating, just very intense. Oh, wow. Breathe, Alexa. He's just a man.

Heat pooled in her cheeks. His gaze sharpened. Great. That's exactly what she needed, for him to know how much he affected her.

"Mrs. Hostetler," a voice called from the doorway. An older man with graying dark hair and kind brown eyes smiled at the group. "Your husband's awake."

The doctor's entrance pulled Gavin's gaze away from her. She sighed. Saved by the doctor.

"Mrs. Hostetler," Gavin said, "would it be all right if I came with you? I want to ask him if he noticed anything that might help us find the man who shot him."

"*Jah*, you may come and ask your questions. If he is not too tired."

Gavin looked back at Alexa. His gaze was focused on the hunt now. "I'll be back in a few. Okay?"

"Absolutely. You go on. I'll be fine here."

He opened his mouth. Then shut it. She was curious about what he'd planned to say, but let it go as he spun on his heel and followed the doctor and Naomi. A moment later, she saw a security guard move to stand right inside the room.

Annoyance mingled with a warm burst of pleasure. Annoyance at the need to be guarded. Pleasure that Gavin had taken a moment to see to her safety. It had been years since anyone worried about her well-being.

Stop it! She shook her head hard, trying to shake his effect on her. She'd been shattered when Brett died. And though she knew he'd not intended to leave her, it had cemented what she already knew. People left you. Her father hadn't even waited until the stamp on his divorce papers had dried before he'd completely abandoned her and her mother, starting over with a newer, better family. She hadn't heard from him in years. Allen had already been out of the house by that time. It had quickly become apparent that he didn't have time to waste on a bratty sister who was ten years younger than he was. Then her mother had died when she was eighteen, a freshman in college.

She slammed her eyes shut, trying to block out the memories of her mother's death. Therapy had helped, but the sense of betrayal was still there.

As was the realization that she hadn't been enough of a reason to stay. For any of them.

Allowing herself to fall for Gavin would be a mistake her heart couldn't afford to make. It would cost her more than she could deal with when he rejected her, too.

"Alexa? I'm ready to go." Gavin approached her. "Everything okay?"

Opening her eyes, she frowned at him. "I'll cope." *I always do.* "I'm ready to get my car and go home."

He returned her frown with interest. Was he irritated or concerned?

"I'm a little uneasy with the idea of you being alone in your house. However, Parker sent me a text a little while ago. Your neighbors have all been there for over three years, so chances of any of them being your stalker are slim. None of them have seen anything suspicious. Which is good news. We're going to be monitoring your house, you know, driving by every couple of hours. And you have a neighborhood crime watch, so they'll be looking out for you, too."

"Good to know."

He hesitated. "You know, what Naomi said? I do believe it. That God is there for us. I'll be praying for you. Just saying."

Ducking his head, he flushed and shifted his stance. Well, that was a surprise. He seemed so confident, but obviously speaking so openly was uncomfortable for him. It touched her that he went there for her. Even if she was a stranger. Or didn't share his faith.

"Thanks, Gavin. I don't have anything against prayer." She lifted her shoulders in a shrug. It seemed inadequate. All at once, the reality of her situation hit. She felt as if she was going to break into pieces if she didn't move. "I just want to go home. Could we go get my car? Please?"

He slanted a level stare toward her. She could almost see the thoughts running through his brain. To her relief, he didn't argue with her.

"Yeah. Let's get out of here."

The breath she'd been holding whooshed from her lungs. Finally.

An hour later, she was sitting in her own blue Ford Focus, driving carefully down the plowed streets to her house. The steady beam of Gavin's headlights in her rearview mirror brought comfort and the false feeling of security. He'd be leaving once they arrived at her place.

Her stomach growled. Had it really been that long since she'd eaten in the police station? Obviously, it had. It was dark now. And it was past her normal dinner hour. If it weren't for the fact that she needed to eat for her health, she'd be willing to skip supper and just crawl into bed. Anything just to make today go away.

Not that tomorrow would be any better.

With that uplifting thought, she pulled into her driveway. Her house was dark. She shivered. On a normal day, she'd be home by now. She'd never minded the dark before.

Now all she could think about was that someone could be waiting inside for her. Her car door was heavy as she swung it open. She didn't even have a garage to provide her some sort of shelter.

Gavin stepped up beside her, resting his hand on the top of the door as she emerged from the warmth of the vehicle into the frigid December evening. He had a flashlight out and swung it around, surveying the property line.

A second cruiser swerved in next to the curb. A female cop exited the vehicle. "Hey, Gavin. Lieutenant Tucker told the chief you needed someone to drive by the place on a regular basis. I saw y'all pull in and thought I would check in with you."

Gavin flashed her a tired smile. "Hey, Zee. I'm about to sweep the perimeter. You want to stay with Alexa here? I don't want her to go into the house until I know it's safe, nor do I want her to hang out here alone."

"Sure thing."

Gavin held out his hand. "Give me your keys. I will check the house, too."

Wordlessly she handed them over, her eyes following him as he jogged off into the darkness. When he was no longer visible, she turned to find herself the object of intense speculation by the female cop. What had he called her? Zee? Did being a cop mean no one went by their actual first name?

The woman's casual demeanor dropped. She was all business now, although her manner remained kind. "Hi, Alexa. I'm Sergeant Claire Zerosky. Let's get you out of the cold. Why don't you pop back into your car for a few minutes until Jackson comes back for you?"

It sounded way too cozy the way she said it. Until he comes back for you. People didn't come for her, though. They never did.

She lost track of how long she waited until he was back. Before she knew it, he was escorting her inside and Claire Zerosky was getting back into her car. She expected him to take off, too.

Therefore, she was taken by surprise when he took off his coat. His sharp eyes moved around her home. Missing very little, she had no doubt.

"No Christmas tree or decorations?" he noted. Was it a question or a statement?

Self-conscious, she shrugged. "It didn't seem to be worth the trouble. It's just me here."

To her relief, he let the subject go.

"Let's get you something to eat. Go ahead and test your blood sugar. It won't bother me. I've been around it before."

She'd guessed as much.

Taking him at his word, she went through her normal routine, hooking up the tester to her phone with a cord. She barely even felt it anymore when the small needle pricked her finger. She looked at the number on the display and sighed in relief. Her numbers, despite the stress of the day, seemed to be up to normal levels.

"Numbers good, huh?"

Her head whipped up. Her eyes widened. Gavin had raided her fridge and was putting a salad together for her. Although she protested, he waved her words away and proceeded to fix the rest of her meal. Deep inside, she was relieved.

She felt better as soon as she'd eaten.

Until he headed for the door.

He turned to her before he left, his eyes intent. "I want you to lock this door behind me and keep it locked. When can you have a dead bolt installed?"

"I can stop by the hardware store after work—"

Uh-oh. Wrong answer. Gavin's black eyebrows lowered until they were scrunched together. He scowled.

"Are you really going to work tomorrow after all that has happened? It's not safe for you. And it could be dangerous for others."

Raising her hands defensively, she gave in. "All right. All right. Tomorrow the clinic's only open until noon, anyway. But I will have to go in on Friday."

"We'll see."

Face grim, he stalked out the door. She locked it behind him. The locks did feel pretty flimsy. Anyone could break in if they really wanted to.

Crawling into bed, she snuggled deep under the electric blanket. She was so cold, she had it turned on high. Her hearing seemed to be amplified. The small noises she never noticed were all crashing in on her sensitive nerves. Her heart was pounding.

For hours she lay awake, shivering under the warmth of her blankets.

If she could just hold on until morning.

Finally, she slept. When she woke up, she wasn't in the best mood. It was a good thing that she had agreed to stay home, she thought. Going in to work would have been difficult.

Zee arrived at about ten, dead bolts in hand. Touched by the gesture, Alexa invited her in.

"I'm not sure if I have all the tools we'll need to install that, Sergeant." Alexa shut the door behind the female sergeant.

Sergeant Zee laughed. "Call me Claire. No worries about the tools. I probably have what we need in the car. I meant to grab them."

As it turned out, Alexa had everything they needed. After reading through the directions together, they got to work.

The two women chatted while they installed the dead bolts on the front and back doors. It was mostly superficial chatter, but it felt good to talk with another woman.

"That's better," Alexa said aloud after she had locked the dead bolt behind Claire. The only one there to hear her was the cat. She laughed, feeling some of the stress drain away. The dead bolts added a sense of safety. Some of the heaviness lifted again.

She puttered around the house after lunch. Placing her newly folded laundry in her dresser, she sat on the couch to read a book that Megan had lent her. When she found out it was an inspirational romance, she almost put it down. Except she was curious now. What was it about God that made people like Gavin put their faith in Him? Should she ask him about it? She shifted uncomfortably. Would he think less of her if he knew she'd never opened a Bible before? Or been to church other than weddings and funerals?

What did it matter what he thought? It wasn't like the man was going to be a permanent fixture in her life.

Turning her back on those worries, she opened her book again almost defiantly. And was sucked into the story. She read a couple of chapters, then her cell phone pinged. She glanced up. And screamed.

Someone was staring through her window.

No news was good, right?

For the hundredth time, Gavin chastised himself for not checking in with Alexa before he arrived to work that morning. Just to prove to himself that she was fine. Each time, he'd try to convince himself that he'd know if she wasn't. Zee had driven past her house several times during the night, and she'd talked to Alexa that morning before going off duty.

It wasn't the same as calling her himself, though.

At least he knew that she hadn't gone to work. That was something. He felt bad about it, but it couldn't be helped. Gavin leaned sideways in his chair and pulled his cell phone out of his back pocket. It was only ten minutes until five in the evening. He wouldn't be able to rest until he'd seen Alexa face-to-face and knew all was well with her. He didn't ask himself why it was so important that he be the one to speak with her. It could have been done by any officer. And he was supposed to be off the clock.

If only Noah Hostetler could have given him

something to go on, maybe he could relax. As it was, Noah had nothing to give him on the shooter.

Grabbing his coat, he shrugged into it as he stalked out of the office. The parking lot was slick. At least the snow had dwindled to a light flurry. He could handle that. In his impatience, he wanted to run to his car. Instead, he was forced to walk slowly so as not to fall and embarrass himself.

The drive to Alexa's house was equally frustrating. The plows and salt trucks were out, but they were a bit behind with their snow removal efforts. What would normally be a ten-minute drive was going to take almost twenty.

He was within a few blocks when his phone rang. It was Alexa's number. His gut knotted. Why was she calling? Was something wrong? Despite the fact that he'd been waiting for her to call all day, a feeling of dread poolcd in the pit of his stomach. He punched the button to put the call on speaker.

"Alexa? What's wrong?"

"Gavin?" He winced at the quaver in her voice. His concern went up a notch. "Someone was looking in my window. He was staring at me!"

"Get away from the windows! I'm two minutes away."

He flipped the switch to turn on his siren and set his lights flashing. The cars in front of him slowed and pulled over. He moved ahead of them, muttering a prayer for her safety as he traveled.

The last mile and a half of the trip took forever. Finally, he arrived, pulling into the short driveway. As he hopped out of the car, the front door opened. The light from inside the house surrounded Alexa, giving the impression that she was glowing.

"Go inside," he ordered. "I'm going to take a look around."

He waited until she had complied, then circled the house. There were indeed footprints by her kitchen windows. The curtains were closed now. Had they been earlier? The prints in the snow circled the house. The stalker had been watching her for more than a few minutes.

He was bold, that was for sure. And determined.

Alexa Grant was in grave danger.

He had his hand raised to knock when the door was yanked open. Alexa grabbed his arm and pulled him inside the house.

"Did you see him? I was so scared! Who was it?"

He held up his hands to stem the flow of questions, shaking his head. "Easy. No, I didn't see him. But I did find footprints beneath your kitchen windows and all the way around your house. I think a police cruiser driving by won't be enough to deter your stalker."

To his surprise, she merely nodded. He'd expected an argument. "I nearly had a heart attack when I saw someone peeking in. I was reading to help myself relax, and I looked up and he was there. But I couldn't get a good look. It was already getting dark out. I saw a shadow, but no face. And glasses. I think he was wearing glasses." She hugged her arms around his waist. "It was a good thing you were so close."

Startled by her sudden embrace, Gavin stood still for a moment. He had no idea what to do. Comforting damsels in distress was not his forte. He reached out and gave her an awkward pat on her shoulder. Should he say something? His mind was a blank. A hint of fragrance rose from her hair, distracting him. It wasn't a heavy perfume scent, but a subtle floral. Just a trace. But enough to catch his attention. It suited her.

Whoa. Where had that thought come from?

This wasn't going to work. Clearing his throat, he patted her shoulder one last time then backed up. Her arms dropped. She wrapped them around herself. He watched the tide of red creep up her cheeks.

Ouch. The last thing he'd wanted to do was to embarrass her. He wasn't cut out to deal with this kind of stuff. Probably why Lacey had preferred his suave brother over socially awkward Gavin.

"So what now?" she asked, still not meeting his eyes.

"Alexa, look at me." He kept his voice soft, willing her to glance up.

Slowly her eyes rose to his. Man, she was pretty. "Yes?"

"I will keep you safe. I will find this guy, whoever he is. And I will put him behind bars." He knew better than to make empty promises. But these promises he meant with all his being. He would do whatever he needed to protect her.

Her lips tilted in a smile. It wasn't reflected in her eyes, but he appreciated the effort. Reaching out, he squeezed her arm.

"Right," he said, releasing her. "I need to

call the station and give an update. We need to start searching the neighborhood."

Before the stalker disappeared again.

He radioed the call in. Within a minute, his radio began beeping. The dispatcher's voice broke through the static. When the address was stated over the radio, Alexa rubbed her hands over her face.

"It's very unsettling hearing an emergency call at your own address."

He smiled at the dry tone in Alexa's voice. She was handling the situation well, but it couldn't have been easy. "I'm sure it is."

A rusty, reluctant chuckle slipped from her. "I will never again complain about being bored. Having nothing going on is a good thing."

He laughed with her. Somehow, he doubted that she complained very much. She didn't seem like she allowed herself the luxury of sharing her thoughts and feelings that much. Kind of like him.

Her stomach growled.

He stood straighter. "It's dinnertime. You need to eat."

She pushed herself to her feet. "Better than sitting and waiting for something else to happen."

Following her to the kitchen, he watched her

begin to search for something to eat. When it became clear, however, that she wasn't feeling up to making anything too fancy, he stepped in. No way was he going to have a diabetic emergency on his hands on top of everything else. Ignoring her protests, he clamped his hands on her shoulders and maneuvered her to the table.

"You rest. I got it covered."

Within a few minutes, he had a simple but hearty dinner in front of her. She narrowed her eyes but obliged him by taking a bite. He smiled. It was amazing how much pleasure it gave him just to see her eat a healthy meal.

Swallowing, she reached for her water and took a sip. "You seem very comfortable doing this." She waved her hand over the food.

"I've had practice. My uncle Leo had type two diabetes. I lived with him for a couple of years after college. He didn't take care of himself, and his numbers got way out of hand. I made it my business to make sure his diabetes was under control again." Allowing his thoughts to dwell on his uncle, his chest tightened briefly. He scowled. "He was a cop."

"Is that why you became a cop?"

"Yeah. He was the person I most admired." His lips twitched into a smile. Uncle Leo had been so proud when he'd graduated from the academy. "I used to drive him crazy with questions about the police force. Back when I first lived with him, I thought that being a cop sounded pretty glamorous. It's not. There's a lot of details and reports. And sometimes, things get dangerous for no reason at all. But I like to think that I'm doing something that matters. Uncle Leo always said that was the important thing to remember. Always make your actions matter."

"What about your parents?"

The smile melted. The warmth in his heart chilled. He wasn't ready to discuss that. Some wounds were best left alone.

He shoved himself away from the counter he'd been leaning against. "Eat up, Alexa. It's going to be a long night."

Hopefully, one that ended without anyone getting hurt. Or worse.

FIVE

Within half an hour, flashlights were circling outside. Every now and then, Gavin would look across the street and see curious neighbors and onlookers standing on the sidewalk. Cars would drive by and slow down, the drivers twisting their necks to get a good look at what was going on.

It wouldn't surprise him if there was an accident in front of Alexa's house thanks to all the rubberneckers. He snorted in disgust. People needed to mind their own business. Deliberately he turned his back to the street, forcing himself to concentrate on finding something, anything, that could lead to Alexa's stalker.

As he'd expected, there wasn't much to find. The footprints were smaller than his own size ten and a half. Probably about a nine, if he had to guess. Unfortunately, shoe size alone didn't reveal any suspects.

It was going on eight by the time the search was completed. The snow was completely trampled, footprints blending together. There was no point in continuing to look. Chief Kennedy sent the other officer on scene, Sergeant Miles Olsen, home to his pregnant wife, while he finished up with Gavin, who had a lot of respect for his boss. Chief Kennedy was honest, fair and thorough. He was a man of his word who was firmly dedicated to serving the people of LaMar Pond.

In a low voice, Gavin related all that he had found out to his boss. The chief whistled. "That's an awful lot for one person to handle. I don't think she should stay here by herself."

Gavin nodded, frustrated. "Agreed. But where would she go? Her only family is a brother, but she refuses to go there. I'm trying to convince her to stay home from work. She said that they are very short-staffed right now."

"I will see what I can come up with in the morning. For now, I am going to put on officer on duty here. I want you to bring her into my office tomorrow morning first thing. She may not like it, but she can't go to work. Let's see if we can come up with a plan."

"Yes, sir." He hesitated. Then decided to ask.

"Chief, is everything okay with Irene? I'm not trying to pry," he hurried to add.

Chief Kennedy smiled and bounced once on his toes. The air of glee around the man was almost tangible. Which was totally out of character. "She's fine, Jackson. Great. Y'all are going to find out soon enough, so I might as well tell you. Irene's pregnant again."

Wow. He hadn't expected that. "You're going to be a dad?"

"Jackson," the chief said, shaking his head in mock reprimand, "I'm already a dad."

Alarmed at his mistake, Gavin quickly tried to fix his error. "Yes, sir. I know that. I didn't mean to imply—"

"Relax, Sergeant. I'm just having fun with you. I know what you meant."

He should just let it go. Gavin knew that. But suddenly he wondered how Irene's two boys, AJ and Matthew, would feel about the new kid? Would they feel like they were second best? Somehow less than the new child? He knew that feeling all too well. Feeling like he was walking a very tight line, he decided to speak his mind. "Please don't take this wrong way, sir. I know you're a good dad. I've seen you with AJ and Matthew, and it's obvious you think the world of them."

How to proceed?

The chief nodded, his expression neutral. "Go ahead, Jackson. Speak your mind."

"I just want to say, it's really important that they know that just because there's going to be a new baby in the house, it doesn't mean that they are loved less. They need to be reassured that because they're stepchildren doesn't mean they are less your kids than the new one."

He puffed out his cheeks, then let the breath whoosh out of him, knowing he'd overstepped. He could not regret it though. Not if it helped those boys grow up knowing their worth. Not like he had. Although, he hadn't been a step-child. But he did know what it was like to be constantly in a sibling's shadow. Sam had always been the child who garnered the majority of their parents' attention. He excelled in everything he did. Sports. Academics. Gavin could recall hearing his parents say that they expected great things from Sam. They were so proud of him.

"What about Gavin?" they'd been asked.

His dad had just shrugged.

It didn't matter if his parents thought he was second best. God loved him. Even with his flaws. Even if no one else valued him, he knew God did. That was enough.

Instead of telling him to mind his own business, the chief gave him a deep look, one that told Gavin his chief heard more than he'd said. Certainly, more than he was comfortable with the man knowing. "Jackson, I hear you. I also agree with you. That's why Irene and I have decided that I will adopt the boys. They will always know of Tony, but I will be their father. I already love them as much as if they were my own flesh and blood."

Shoving his hands into his pockets, Gavin ducked his head briefly and cleared his throat. "Right. I will bring Alexa by in the morning."

The chief smiled, clearly not fooled. Gavin was relieved when the man went along with the subject change.

Gavin went into the house to talk to Alexa. She wasn't going to like what he had to say, but that was just too bad. Her safety, and the safety of those at the clinic, had to come first.

Five minutes later, he found her inside, talking with Zee. The two women were speaking in low voices.

"Ladies, may I interrupt to speak with Alexa for a few minutes?"

Both women looked at him. While Zee gave him her usual smile, Alexa's gaze was considerably cooler. Uh-oh. He recalled the way he'd refused to answer her question earlier, before the others arrived. He knew his tone of voice had been abrupt. If he had to guess, she was still upset with him about that. He held back the wince that wanted to form on his face. He was here to investigate a crime, not to protect her feelings. Or to discuss his past.

That didn't mean he needed to be rude, though. He sighed. There was no way around it. He'd have to apologize.

"Sure, Jackson. I need to go talk to the chief anyways." Zee left the room.

Silence descended. It was thick.

"Alexa, I apologize if I was rude before. One thing you'd know if you knew me better is that I tend to be abrupt. Nothing personal."

She rolled her eyes. "That's not much of an apology. But I suppose I shouldn't have asked something personal. I know you're here to protect me and to find the guy who's after me. Not to be my friend and hold my hand."

Actually, the idea of holding her hand had its appeal.

What? No. Absolutely not. He was not going there.

"Glad we got that cleared up. The chief wants you in his office in the morning. We need to see what we can find out about your stalker."

"What you're really telling me is that work tomorrow is out of the question." There was no inflection in her voice. He couldn't tell if she was agreeing or asking him.

"Exactly. Yeah." He stood quietly, waiting to see what her response would be.

She surprised him. Moving to the window, she lifted a slat on the blind and peered out. From the back, he saw the muscles in her shoulders tighten. The finger holding the slat shook slightly.

"What do I do if he comes back tonight, Gavin?"

Her voice was soft, but he could still hear the tremor layered beneath it. She was terrified and doing her best to keep it under wraps.

"Lexie." He stepped closer. Her shoulders tightened even more. "I won't lie to you. He's still out there somewhere. But the chief is putting an officer right outside all night. We might end up moving you, even. For now, though, you aren't going to be left alone."

"Why'd you call me that?"

Huh? He'd expected a question about what he told her, not that. What had he called her? Lexie. Oh yeah. *You don't give people you're protecting pet names.* Too late. He shrugged. "Lexie? I don't know. It just slipped out. Sorry."

She moved a quarter turn, so that her face was in profile. It was hard to see her features. They were in the shadows. "It's all right. I don't mind. My grandfather used to call me that. When I was a kid. He died when I was nine."

"If it bothers you—"

"It's fine." Visibly shaking herself out of her mood, she released the slat. It settled back into place with a click. "So I need to call in tomorrow. Fine. Dr. Quinton will probably fire me, but hey, it's just a job."

He couldn't tell if she was serious or not. "Sorry, but that's the way it has to be. For now." If only there was something else he could do for her.

"Gavin, can I ask you something?"

He glanced back at her, surprised at the hesitant tone of her voice. "Yeah. Go ahead. What do you want to know?"

He assumed it was about the case, or about the protection detail. He was wrong.

"At the hospital, you told Naomi that you put your trust in God. Were you being serious?"

That was not what he expected. However, he believed that one should never miss an opportunity to witness, especially when the person asked.

"Absolutely I was being serious. God has helped me through some pretty tough times."

"But why? Is it because that was the way you were raised?"

"I wasn't raised in a Christian home, if that's what you want to know. Growing up, we were pretty much Christmas and Easter churchgoers. We went 'cause it was the thing to do. But Uncle Leo, man, he believed and trusted God with his whole heart. So when I moved in with him, I got to know God, too. Started reading the Bible for the first time in my life. It brought me hope."

Her eyes kindled. "Hope. I could use some of that."

His phone rang. He turned away to answer it. "Jackson."

"Sergeant, I have the house covered for the night. You need to have Miss Grant in my office at eight thirty sharp. I have the visual artist, Tara, scheduled for nine."

"Yes, sir. Will do." He disconnected the phone and gave her the message. She nodded but didn't say anything. When the night officer pulled up outside, Gavin went out to greet him. The house was encased in shadows. She needed security lights. Gavin ambled over to greet the officer on watch. *He's a good cop.*

The reminder didn't help him feel better about leaving her in someone else's care. Would anyone else be watching the house tonight?

Gavin wondered just how far the stalker was willing to go to get to the woman inside the house.

Alexa just wanted to go to sleep and wake up to find it was all a dream.

After Brett's death, she'd worked hard to pull her life together again. No longer feeling welcome at the hospital she'd worked in because of the rumors and the cold shoulder she was getting from her colleagues, she decided to move. She'd never been a fan of the big city. She and Brett had planned to move to a more suburban area after they were married.

Knowing she needed to move, she had begun to search online for job openings. When she saw a job posted for a position that would entail working in a clinic with additional shifts in the local hospital, she had decided to apply. She'd never been to Pennsylvania but felt she couldn't be choosey. When she'd arrived in LaMar Pond for her interview, though, she'd been enchanted by the small-town feel of the place.

The dull ache in her chest was a reminder

of what she'd lost. It wasn't as sharp as it had been. The pain had lost some of its strength, but she knew that she'd never forget Brett. Part of her wondered if it hurt this bad to lose a fiancé, how much worse would it have been to lose a husband? Or a child? Was that really a situation she wanted to put herself in?

Would she be able to survive such a situation?

She didn't think she'd ever find out. The idea of falling in love and getting married no longer held the thrall it once had. She was better off alone. Maybe she was lonely, but she was fine with that. She had a cat for company and a job she loved. What else did she need?

She ignored the niggle in her heart that laughed at her, saying she was fooling herself.

Footsteps in the kitchen brought her up off the couch where she'd been sitting. Gavin walked into the room. The intense energy that buzzed around him was invigorating. But even as she felt better just being in his presence, she couldn't help but note how exhausted he was. His black hair was standing on end, no doubt because he'd been running his hand through it. His eyes were drooping.

A huge yawn stretched his mouth wide. He quickly covered it with his hand, but not soon enough. She ducked her head to hide her smile. She wouldn't want to offend him by laughing.

"Hey, Lexie. Don't laugh at me."

She laughed anyway, especially when he gave her a ridiculous grin.

Her laughter died off at his next words. "I think that I have done everything I can here. I need to head home before I can't function anymore. A police car just pulled up outside."

"A police car is going to be there for the whole night, right?"

He nodded, yawning again. "Yep. Don't worry. You won't be alone. Tomorrow I'll swing by and pick you up around eight." He grabbed up his jacket, which he'd slung over the back of a kitchen chair. He shrugged into it. "You going to be okay?"

She refused to give in to the weak impulse to say, no, she wouldn't be fine. "Of course. There's an officer outside. I'll be fine."

Ten minutes later, she wished she'd given in to her impulse. Every sound seemed to be amplified. The wind, the cars driving past, even a dog barking. To her hypersensitive ears, each sound seemed to come from right outside her door. Every ten minutes or so, she'd peek out the corner of the front blinds to check that the police car was still parked in her driveway.

Stop it! she ordered herself. *No one is going to pull any stunts when a cop car is parked outside the house.* Fortified by the thought, she decided to go to bed early. She double-checked the door locks and the dead bolts. All sealed. She should be safe inside. Refusing to ponder who she was trying to convince, she hurried through her nightly routine. Teeth brushed and in her comfy pajamas, she went to bed.

And soon found that her mind refused to shut off and allow her to sleep. Every time she shut her eyes, the image of Noah crumpling to the ground, or of a face peering through her window would flash through her mind and her eyes would pop open again. After forty minutes of tossing and turning, she gave up and decided to do something productive.

Going to the living room, she picked up her laptop and turned it on. After an hour, she felt her eyes grow heavy again. Laying her laptop aside, she pulled a fleece blanket around herself. She grunted softly as her large orange cat, Cinnamon, leaped up onto her feet and decided to make himself comfortable. When he settled in and started to purr, she hated to move him. Plus, the familiar rumble on her feet was comforting.

I'll go upstairs in a few minutes.

She didn't move. Every time she thought about moving upstairs, she shuddered. If she went upstairs, anyone could enter her house and she wouldn't know until it was too late.

She waited, wondering if anyone was out there watching her right now.

Alexa jerked awake. She'd drifted to sleep despite her terror. Meowing angrily, Cinnamon jumped down from the sofa.

What had woken her up? The room was dark. The house was silent, with the exception of the pounding of her pulse in her ears. Was someone in the house with her?

She couldn't hear anything. Gently, cautiously, she eased off the couch. Her toes curled into the carpet as she placed her feet on the floor. Standing, she slowly walked toward the window. She grabbed the edge of the blind and gently eased up one slat. Peeking outside, she breathed a sigh of relief. The police car was still outside. She could see a light on inside it. He must have been looking at his phone. A sliver of the fear inside her uncurled and melted away. She wasn't alone.

She had been silly to worry. She still had no idea what time it was, although it was still night. For once, she wished she had a digital clock in the living room instead of a small oval clock with hands that was hanging on the wall. At least then she'd be able to tell the time without turning on any lights. If she turned one on, the officer might see it and come to check on her. She hated being a bother.

But she also hated not knowing what time it was.

Huffing a sigh, she gave in. Flipping on a switch, she looked to the opposite side of the room to gaze at the clock. Four o'clock. She'd be getting up in another hour and a half anyway. She might as well just stay awake.

Leaving the light on, Alexa started to pivot.

Fear rooted her to the spot.

Blinking, hoping she was seeing things, she looked again. A whimper escaped her mouth.

There, on the couch, right next to where her head had been minutes before, was a single red rose.

How had she not knocked it off the couch when she got up?

A sound caught her attention. Whirling, she squinted into the darkness. A shadow moved, came closer. She could make out the silhouette of a person. He was around her height. He had something around his head. A hood or a scarf. But she could see the gleam of his eyes.

Her stalker was here, inside her house.

Screaming, she turned and tried to run. She didn't get far. Strong arms wrapped around her and yanked her back. A harsh, whispered laugh assaulted her senses. She could feel his breath on her ear. Terror whirled in her brain. She didn't want to die.

"Where are you going, Alexa?" Her unwelcome guest hissed. The voice was vaguely familiar, but she couldn't place it. Not disguised within that guttural whisper. "We were meant to be together. I can't allow you to keep betraying me."

She was not going to die, she thought furiously. Not now. He wasn't much taller than she was. Banging her head back against him, she heard a grunt and a surprised exclamation. She had to get out of the house now.

Slamming her foot into his shin forced the man to loosen his grip. Alexa wriggled free and made it to the door. She was slipping outside when his hands grabbed her hair. She didn't stop. A few strands ripped from her head. Ignoring the pain, she ran outside in her bare feet. Right through small piles of snow. She barely felt the cold. The cop on duty met her on the driveway. She could see his gun was drawn.

"He's inside my house!" she gasped.

"Wait here," he ordered. Then he darted inside. A few minutes later, the officer was back. "He ran out the back. I'm calling it in."

Alexa could hardly stand up. How would she ever feel safe again? And where could she go that this man wouldn't be able to find her?

SIX

Gavin woke up when his cell phone rang, his heart pounding. He glanced at the clock. Four in the morning. Phone calls at 4:00 a.m. were never a good thing. Something must have happened to Lexie. Echoes of sirens and situations that had gone bad filled his mind.

No! He couldn't afford to get distracted. Lexie needed him to stay focused. He had to keep his emotions, his heart, uncluttered so that he could save her life. That was all that mattered.

Snatching the phone off the end table next to his bed, he barked into the phone, "Yeah?"

A moment's pause.

"Jackson, it's Mac." Hearing his colleague's voice on the other end of the call made the hair on the back of his neck stand on end.

He knew it! Something was wrong. He should have stayed with Lexie.

"Miss Grant is fine, but there's been an incident."

"An incident? Explain that, Mac."

Settle down, man. Stay calm. He'd gone way beyond that point. The woman had gotten under his skin in less than forty-eight hours. He'd make sure she was safe, put her stalker in jail, then he'd deal with the repercussions.

"She ran out of the house a while ago. Seems the stalker had gone in while she was sleeping and left a rose."

"You touch the rose?"

"No, man. Of course not. I'm not a rookie." The slight hint of disgust in Mac's voice almost made him smile. Almost. "There's more. He was still in the house. He got away, but he made a grab for her. I don't know what his intent was. I did call the chief. And she insisted I call you."

Warmth flooded him. She'd asked for him. Wait. That didn't matter. But he still stood up and started grabbing his gear. It was imperative that he get there right away.

"I'm on my way."

Hanging up before Mac could say anything else, he made record time in getting ready. Only a few minutes had passed since he ended the phone call when he backed out of his parking space. It had snowed again. His high beams sliced through the air, highlighting lacy flakes drifting down. It was picturesque. The glistening white snow together with the Christmas lights and decorations. Beautiful. And so out of sync with the terror of the scene he was traveling to.

He thought Alexa might be a mess when he got there. To his relief, she wasn't.

"I can't stay here." Alexa met him at the door with that statement. She was holding the largest cat he'd ever seen. It overflowed her arms, nailing him with a suspicious feline stare.

"I know you can't, Lexie." He turned to Mac. He didn't even ask if Mac had fallen asleep on the job. The idea of that happening was outrageous. "How'd he get in?" Gavin knew the dead bolts were in place. Zee had sent him a text about them that afternoon.

"None of the doors were breached. I found new footprints in the back of the house. It looks like he forced one of the basement windows open. It wasn't broken, but the lock had rusted."

The windows. He'd checked all of them. Except for the basement ones.

Gavin let the other officers work the scene. His gaze caught Lexie's. Held it. She stared at him like he was a life raft and she was drowning. In a way, she must have thought she was. "Show me the rose."

Without a word, she jerked her chin, motioning him to follow her. Her steps dragged a bit. The cat leaped to the floor. She crossed her now-empty arms and rubbed her hands along them. Gavin took a step closer, hoping his presence brought her some comfort. She didn't seem to notice. In the living room, his blood chilled. She'd clearly been sleeping on the couch. He took it all in. The bunched-up fleece flung to the one end of the couch. The two pillows that had spilled onto the floor. The laptop settled on the end table.

And the bloodred rose on a pristine white cushion. Right where she'd been.

"Gavin," Lexie whispered.

"Yes?"

"I can't be sure, but I think I have heard his voice before."

He whipped his gaze back to her. "Yeah? Can you remember where?"

She shook her head. "I'm not even positive about it. But there was a familiar quality to it."

He could see the anxiety growing inside her. "If you remember, let me know."

His own level of frustration was growing.

Shifting his emotions to the side was harder than it usually was. Her life depended on his ability to sift through the facts with logic and precision.

Reaching into his jacket pocket, he pulled out the latex gloves and the plastic evidence bag he always carried with him. Blanking the image of Lexie lying on the couch next to the rose from his brain, he slipped on the gloves, then strode to the couch to collect the rose.

"Did you touch it?"

A quick head shake. Nope.

"I didn't want to go anywhere near it."

That was good. She hadn't contaminated it. Much. She might still have touched it when she was moving around.

The sound of a car pulling into the driveway grabbed his attention. Hand on the service weapon at his waist, he moved soundlessly to the window and peered out. A familiar police SUV was parked behind Mac's car. The door opened, and a man in his early thirties stepped out.

"Hey, Lexie. The chief's here."

A moment later, Paul Kennedy was standing beside him as they all took in the scene.

A cell phone pinged in the silence.

"Oh no."

He sure didn't like the tone in her voice.

"Alexa. What's going on?" He kept his voice devoid of any emotion with effort.

"It's him, Gavin. He sent me a text."

"What does it say?" Chief Kennedy asked.

Alexa's voice was trembling as she read the text. "'You've disappointed me again. You shouldn't have called the police. You'll have to be punished for your betrayal.'"

The silence was broken only by the ragged breaths coming from Alexa. Gavin couldn't risk glancing her way, knowing she was crying. If he saw her tears, he didn't think he'd be able to handle it.

"Sergeant, I want you to get Miss Grant to the station. For her own safety. When we're finished here, I will join you."

"Yes, sir." Looking at Alexa, Jackson jerked his head and motioned for her to join him. He didn't trust himself to say anything, not yet. The anger had started to settle, but it wasn't gone.

"My cat." She scooped the cat up in her arms, ignoring its meow of protest. She hugged the large feline closer to her.

He narrowed his eyes at the cat. He couldn't have an animal locked up in his car. The chief responded for him. "Take the cat. You can put him in my office until we get this figured out."

Moving beside Alexa out to his car, he placed the palm of his hand against her back to keep her walking while he continuously shone his flashlight around, searching the surrounding area. But he didn't see anything. He hadn't expected to.

"What are you going to do with it? The rose?" Lexie's voice seemed loud in the silence, even though it was barely above a whisper.

"It's evidence. Hopefully, it will help us locate this creep. We don't have much to go on, even with what Noah Hostetler saw. Right now, anything will help."

Opening the passenger door, he waited for her to slide inside with the cat before he jogged around to his side. As he got in, he saw a shadow moving. He tossed the bag with the rose onto the seat. "Stay here!" he yelled, shutting the door and locking it.

Thumbing his radio, he called in to the chief. "Possible sighting on east side of the house. Victim is in my car. I'm heading in."

"Watch your step, Sergeant," the chief replied. "Mac's coming, too."

He heard the front door open and then muffled steps as Mac raced through the snow. A third person exited. The chief was guarding Alexa in the car.

Good. With her safe, he could act.

He plunged into the darkness and let it swallow him whole as he chased down a stalker. And possibly a killer.

What had Gavin seen?

Alexa tightened her grip on Cinnamon. Narrowing her eyes, she strained to see where he and Mac had gone in the darkness. After they'd taken off, though, the darkness had completely blocked them from her sight. She knew that Chief Kennedy was right outside the vehicle. There shouldn't have been any difference. She should have felt as safe with him as she did with Gavin.

There was a difference, though. A big one. She was growing comfortable with Gavin. Plus, he'd already proved that he was willing to take care of her.

But she didn't need any man to take care of her.

Although right now she sure needed some protection. *How do you fight an attacker when you have no idea what he looks like?*

Cinnamon let out a loud meow.

"Oh! Sorry, Cinnamon! I didn't realize I'd been squeezing you so tight." She relaxed her arms, and the irritated cat crawled majestically off her lap. When he curled up on the driver's seat, she bit her lip. Gavin wouldn't be happy about the cat sitting in his seat. Or on the evidence bag.

A knock on the window made her shriek.

Whipping around, her hand at her throat, she saw Gavin staring in at her. Or rather at the cat on his seat.

Grabbing the cat, she pulled him off the driver's seat. Gavin opened the door and got in, moving the evidence bag out of his way as he sat.

"Sorry!"

He waved away her apology. "No big deal. I have a cat myself."

She blinked. She hadn't pegged him as a cat owner. But thinking about it, it made sense. Cats were very independent animals. A loner like him would appreciate it. Why she thought he was loner, she couldn't say. He just seemed to be someone who didn't let too many people get close to him.

She needed to get back on topic. "Did you find him?"

"No. But I chased him quite a way. He was

wearing dark clothes, but I could tell that he was shorter than me. Probably about five-five or five-six. I lost him when he crossed the train tracks. Seconds in front of an oncoming train. The man has no fear."

The drive to the station was quiet. Between the events of the night and her lack of sleep, Alexa was just too exhausted to hold a proper conversation. She looked over a couple of times at Gavin. His brows were furrowed in thought. Since he made no effort to talk, either, she figured he was thinking about the case.

At the station, he held the door open for her and waited while she gathered the cat before walking inside with her.

After making sure she checked her blood sugar and ate, Jackson sat down across from her. "Obviously, you can't go back to work right now. And just as obvious, you can't go back to your place. We have a safe house for you and Cinnamon there." He jerked his thumb toward the cat seated under a table. "The visual artist, Tara, will be in this morning. In the meantime, we'll just hang out here for her and the chief."

A while later, the visual artist arrived. She was pleasant and asked a lot of good questions designed to jog the memory. However,

Alexa wasn't able to tell her much. Both times she'd seen her stalker, he'd been in shadows and wearing a dark hood. His eyes were dark. That's all she could remember. Well, she'd been able to tell that he had dark hair. But that could have been an illusion. The first night she'd caught a glimpse of dark eyebrows. She'd forgotten about that until Tara had jogged her memory.

"I think that's all we can do for now," Tara said, closing her notebook computer with a click. If she was feeling frustrated, she hid it behind a professional smile. Alexa, on the other hand, wasn't above admitting that she was feeling frustrated.

"I'm sorry I couldn't give you more," she apologized. "Just a pair of eyes. That's not much to go on."

"It's more than we had yesterday." The woman stood and exited the room. Gavin moved from his spot against the wall and sauntered over to her. She glanced up at him, frowning.

"What's wrong?" he asked.

"Oh, nothing. I was just thinking about something. I know that I can't go into the clinic today. But I do have a couple of Amish patients that I need to see at their homes. If you go with me, do you think we could do that?"

It was his turn to frown. "I don't think that's a good idea. Call the clinic and see if someone else can go."

"I don't think there is anyone else—"

He interrupted her, his expression drawing tight. Intense. "You have no idea what this man will do!" Gavin exclaimed. "He has already attacked you and one of your patients. He has sent threatening messages, and it is very likely that he has killed other people in Chicago. Including your fiancé." Gavin's face softened. He strode to her side. Tucked a piece of hair back behind her ear. The side of her face where his finger grazed tingled. "Lexie, you are in serious danger. And you're not making my job of protecting you very easy."

It was the soft way he said her name that made her capitulate. For some reason, it was very important to him. And not just because it was his job.

Grinding her teeth, she tapped out the number on her phone. He was right; she knew he was. But it galled her no end to let some stranger with an agenda have so much control over her life. She put the call on speakerphone. It would save her the time of having to reiterate everything for Gavin's benefit.

It's not about you, Alexa. You have to do what's best for the patients.

Unfortunately, sending another nurse wasn't an option.

"You have to go!" Megan's voice was uncharacteristically rushed, with just a hint of panic. "Our waiting room is full, and our schedule is booked solid today. There is no one else who can go. And you know that Marvin is depending on you."

Alexa groaned. There was nothing like a good case of guilt. She'd have to go. There was no other way. And she would have to convince Gavin to go with her. Disconnecting the call, she faced him again. As expected, he didn't look happy. Actually, that was putting it lightly. He looked downright irritated.

"Is there no way that this Marvin guy can come into the clinic? It would really save us a lot of trouble if you did not have to go on this visit."

"I wish it were possible. If he could, then I wouldn't worry about it at all. However, Marvin has a weak immune system. There's no way we can ask him to come into a waiting room filled with sick people, especially with that nasty influenza virus going around. That would be asking for trouble."

"Fine," he bit out. "I hate this. You know that, right? I would hate to have that man die, though, because you couldn't do your job. But this means you gotta let me do mine. I'm going with you, and if I tell you to do something, I need you to do it immediately, no questions. Got it?"

He stared into her eyes. She nodded.

Apparently satisfied, he stepped back and turned to the door.

"I'll notify the chief, and then we'll get going. The sooner we get there, the sooner we can get back and find a way to keep you safe."

It turned out that convincing the chief was even harder than convincing Gavin. He was gone for a full ten minutes. It was ridiculous, she thought to herself, how nervous she was waiting in the police station. If she just walked outside the door, she was sure to run smack into somebody with a badge and gun. It was the safest place for her to be. And yet, she felt vulnerable.

She was so nervous that when Gavin opened the door, she jumped. Picking up her coat from the rack standing in the corner, he handed it to her. Silently she shrugged into it.

"The chief agreed, but I'm to keep in radio contact with him every step of the way."

"Sounds good."

Within a few minutes, they were in the car and heading out. Gavin kept up a steady stream of banter, to relax her and take her mind off things no doubt, but as much as she tried to focus on the conversation, she couldn't. Instead, she kept finding herself looking into the side mirror.

"Alexa, stop that."

"Stop what?"

Gavin let out a laugh. It was low and warm, and actually held true amusement. Had she heard him really laugh before? Granted, there hadn't been much to laugh about in the short time they'd known each other, but she found herself wanting to hear him laugh again.

"You keep turning to look in the side mirror. It's making me nuts." He threw her a sideways glance. Yep. Definitely amused.

"I can't help it. I keep thinking that this guy could be anyone! I'd never know it."

"You said that you thought his voice sounded familiar, right?"

In her mind, she could hear the low whisper in her ear again. She shivered. The acid in her stomach churned.

"Yeah, but I think he was deliberately trying to sound different. I couldn't place where I thought I knew it from. Sorry."

He sighed. "Lexie, none of this is your fault. Everything that's happened is because of your stalker's choices. He's responsible for his own actions."

"Turn left at the next intersection." She sat straighter as they neared the junction where the two roads met. The cruiser smoothly turned onto the road. It was a state highway, which was a fancy way of saying it was a long, paved, two-lane road with lots of traffic. They passed multiple cars, trucks and several buggies. She grew tenser by the mile as they approached where Marvin King lived.

She squinted as she stared through the front windshield. The sun was out, casting a glare where it reflected off the white snow.

It was a quiet, peaceful morning.

A peace that was shattered by a gunshot.

SEVEN

"Hold on." Gavin pushed his foot on the gas, then hit the radio button to call in the gunshot.

"This is Marvin's place!" Alexa yelled, pointing at a long driveway leading up to a large white farmhouse.

Gavin could just make out a brown, log cabin–styled barn jutting behind the house. The field next to the house was buried under more than a foot of snow. A buggy was parked in the barn. He could see a horse in the back field.

Someone was home.

Hopefully, he'd find them alive and well.

Coming to a full stop beside the house, he unhooked his seat belt. "Stay here. I'm going to check this out."

Without waiting to see if she would obey him, he swung the driver's door open and stepped outside the vehicle. Keeping low, he edged toward the house. His gaze made a full circle around the yard, searching for anything out of the ordinary or suspicious. Nothing. Nothing was good. He took a few more cautious steps toward the house.

Still nothing.

Knowing how the Amish felt about guns and violence, Gavin replaced his service weapon in his holster as he climbed the porch steps and stood at the front door. He kept his hand on the weapon, just in case. He knocked. Waited. Knocked again.

After a minute, he moved away from the door and walked toward the back of the house. The porch was a wraparound. Peering around the corner, he squinted. No one was in sight.

He had a bad feeling about this.

Going back down to the cruiser, he motioned for Lexie to roll down the window. "I'm not getting a response, and no one's in sight. Is it possible he isn't here?"

Her lips tilted down in a puzzled frown. "Not likely. This is a standing appointment with us. If he had an emergency, he would have found a way to call or let the clinic know to get in touch with me."

A fierce light kindled in her eyes. Without warning, she unlatched her seat belt and opened the door with enough force to make him jump back out of the way. She swung her long legs out of the car and stood, hands on her hips. Turning in a full circle, she searched the snow-covered property from the large white farmhouse, to the fields in front, to the woods that ran alongside the back and the north side.

"Hey! Lexie, what are you doing? Get back in the car."

"Something horrible has happened, Gavin. I'm sure of it. Even if Marvin weren't around, his sister Linda would have been here. Or at the very least, she'd have left a note on the front door."

Alexa knew these people. If she believed they were here or in trouble, he had to believe her. He needed to go around the corner and check things out. Leaving Alexa alone and unguarded in the cruiser wasn't an option. He needed to move, though. His gut said that the gunshot they heard came from here, on the property.

Drawing his service weapon again, he motioned for Alexa to step closer. Deliberately placing her between him and the building, he gave her instructions in a low voice.

"Stay next to the house. And next to me.

That gunshot was close to here. We need to find your patient. Now."

Eyes flaring wide, she nodded. The urge to reach out and squeeze her hand in encouragement almost shocked a snort out of him. Yeah, that would be real professional. Not to mention, if her stalker was out here, he'd probably not take too kindly to any evidence of overt friendliness. Not that he seemed to need a reason. A man entering a clinic for health care wasn't exactly a romantic rendezvous.

Now was not the time for conjecture. "Stay low," he hissed at Alexa. She hunched her shoulders and bent her knees. Satisfied, he began to move forward, eyes busily scanning the horizon for any sign of movement.

"What was that?" Alexa's tight voice whispered beside him.

They paused. Gavin held himself rigid, straining his ears to catch any stray sounds.

There. He heard it. It sounded like a groan.

The groan of someone in pain. The noise came from somewhere ahead of them.

Picking up the pace, they reached the back of the house. Beside him, Alexa gasped. Gavin slid his eyes in Alexa's direction. Catching his gaze on her, she raised a shaking arm and pointed to the left.

Gavin's view was obstructed by a large tree. Leaning toward her to see around it, he was able to make out a dark shape in the snow, half hidden by the corner of the barn.

He saw something dark blue, like a pair of dark blue trousers worn by Amish men. And right beside it, a straw hat. The body moved, just a bit. Enough to let them know that he was still alive.

They'd found Marvin King, but it appeared that the stalker had found him first. From this far away, it was impossible to tell how badly he was hurt.

The only way to know for sure was to go over there and check. But the scene was not safe. Using his radio, he called in to check on the status of backup and to let the dispatcher know to send an ambulance.

"Backup on the way, Sergeant," the dispatcher reported. "It should arrive within five minutes."

Five minutes. He really hoped other officers would arrive on scene sooner than that.

"You said his sister would be here somewhere, too?" he asked.

She nodded.

His gut clenched. *Lord, please let her be safe.*

"What are we going to do?" Alexa whispered as he disconnected with the dispatcher.

"Lexie, we can't go over there to him right now. This scene is not safe. If we went over there, we'd be out in the open. *You'd* be out in the open. I don't think whoever is out there would hesitate to take a shot at either one of us."

She sucked in a harsh breath. Although she had to know that what he said was true, she certainly didn't like it. But she didn't argue. It was a bit humbling to realize that she trusted his judgment so completely. Except for his fellow cops, who had ever trusted him that much?

Leo had trusted him. But Leo was dead. And he had to accept some of the blame for that. He slammed down that train of thought. It would do no one any good. But would this beautiful, independent woman see him any differently if she knew how badly he'd failed his uncle?

Suddenly his senses went into hyperdrive. The feeling of being watched slid over him. His shoulders twitched.

"Get down!" he ordered "We're being watched."

Without hesitation, Alexa hit the ground. Snow puffed up from the pile she'd landed on, then drifted down like tiny feathers, landing in her hair and on her clothes. He landed right beside her and raised himself a bit higher. Whoever went after her would have to get through him first.

A chunk of the house shattered, spattering them with debris. She flinched, hard. He could feel her trembling beside him. They'd been shot at sniper style.

Could they survive out here long enough for help to arrive?

Alexa couldn't hear anything over the pounding of her own blood in her ears. Every second she expected to feel a bullet hit her from any direction. Where was the shooter hiding?

Next to her Gavin adjusted his position. Was he hurt? A burst of fear for him shot through her. Moving her head so that she could examine him, she saw that he wasn't injured. His eyes met hers. She could see the question in them. Was she okay? She attempted a smile. All she could pull off was a slight quirk of her lips. She had to hold her mouth tight to still the tremble that wanted to show up.

Apparently, it was enough to reassure Gavin.

He moved again. This time to push the radio on his shoulder to call in the shooting.

He'd just started speaking when another bullet hit the house, this one two inches closer.

Biting back a shriek, Alexa ducked her head. She felt the snow on her chin. The cold was starting to seep into her bones. A third bullet struck the pole of the clothesline with a loud, hollow ping.

"See where the bullet hit the clothesline?" Gavin asked. She looked where his finger pointed. There was a dent in the pole. "He must be shooting from those trees over there." He gestured to the left behind them. "My cruiser is in his way. That's why he can't get a lock on us."

As if to prove his point, the back window of the cruiser shattered. The sound echoed in the winter stillness. Gavin winced.

He lifted his gaze from her to sweep the area again. He was plotting something. Hopefully, it would work. He swung his piercing blue stare back to her. She held on to his eyes with her own, for strength and assurance. If he believed he could get them out of this, she'd believe it, too.

What if she said a prayer? A novel thought, but she was willing to grab on to anything at this point. *Um, God. Hello. Help?* It was the best she had; she hoped it would be enough.

Gavin leaned in closer to her, his words low and intense. "Lexie, can you crawl? I think we might be out of his range if we can crawl around the corner to the back of the house."

She didn't want to move and risk exposing themselves even more. At the same time, if they remained were they were, they would be trapped if the shooter was able to get a better angle. Biting her lip, she nodded.

"Good. Listen, you go ahead of me. Since he's behind us right now, I'll be able to cover you."

She didn't like the sound of that. It was like he expected to be shot.

"Gavin—" She could hardly think of what to say. Terror squeezed her heart in its cold fist. What if he got hurt? Or worse.

He reached out and touched her face. The touch was so gentle, it was like butterfly wings kissing her cheeks.

"You need to go, Lexie. Army crawl to the corner. Now."

Blinking her eyes, she forced herself to face forward, even though every instinct demanded she turn to be sure he was right behind her. Slowly, slowly, she used her elbows and knees to propel herself forward. One foot. Two. It seemed to take forever, but she could see the edge of the house coming closer.

Just a few more feet.

Crack!

The bullet hit right where she'd been a second ago.

"Move, Lexie! He's changed position."

Ceasing all attempts to army crawl, she scrambled to her knees and speed crawled to the corner. Shuffling noises let her know that Gavin was coming up right behind her.

When she reached the corner, she realized she was panting. Pushing herself with a burst of energy, she jumped up and rounded the corner, diving behind the pile of wood that was stacked there. She propped herself up against the white siding. Gavin plopped down beside her. His gun was out, ready in his hand, and he peered around the woodpile. They weren't out of danger. Not yet.

The minutes stretched by. Alexa fully expected the madman to appear at any moment.

Sirens split the air. Both of them slumped back against the house, knowing that help had arrived. The sounds of multiple vehicles pulling up along the road and onto the driveway reached them. Within moments, Sergeant

Parker and another officer were combing the woods. Paramedics were seeing to Marvin. He wasn't dead, but he was in critical condition. Between his illness and the wound, it would be touch and go for a while.

Where was Linda?

Parker and the other officer, Lieutenant Willis, returned from searching the area.

"Parker." Gavin sauntered over to the officers, his expression tense. Unwilling to be left out, Alexa jogged behind him. "What do ya know?"

"We didn't find the shooter, if that's what you're asking," Parker said. Disappointed, she felt herself droop a bit with sudden fatigue. "Nor did we find the sister. But we did find footprints. They were all trampled together, so it was impossible to tell if they were all made by the same feet or if there was more than one person."

After another minute of conversation, the officers went to continue searching the property. Gavin and Alexa watched the paramedics load Marvin onto a stretcher. His eyes were closed. There was no telling how he was doing from where they stood.

"I feel like this is all my fault." The words

slipped out. She hadn't planned on speaking them. But they were true, all the same.

She started when Gavin took her hand in his. When they'd first met, he hadn't seemed the type to hold a girl's hand in comfort. There were so many things she'd been wrong about.

"This is not your fault, Lexie. I'm sorry that your patient was hurt. But we will find the man responsible. It's my number-one priority right now."

"Hey, Jackson. You are going to want to come and see this." A paramedic stood near where Marvin had lain. Gavin released her hand. She immediately wanted to reach out and grab hold of his again. Which was ridiculous. He had a job to do.

Gavin walked past her, giving her shoulder a gentle squeeze on the way. It was amazing, but even after all that had happened, that one simple gesture brought tears to her eyes and filled some of the cold spaces inside her with warmth.

Which didn't mean that she was going to stand there feeling sentimental. The stalker was chasing her, after all. Straightening her shoulders, she followed Gavin, ignoring the questioning look on the paramedic's face. Gavin, at least, didn't protest her presence.

However, he gave her a look taut with concern. Dread shivered up her spine. What was that expression about?

She looked down. There, on the ground, amid the white snow dotted with Marvin King's blood, was a red rose.

EIGHT

Alexa was worn out. Never in her life had she been this tired. And she'd been plenty tired and discouraged before. The difference, though, was that the pain and anguish of having others leave her and reject her, while very real, had never threatened her life. Or the life of those she cared about. Now, in the space of a few days, she'd had two patients attacked, an acquaintance go missing and Gavin had been put in the way of danger several times. Not to mention the fact that someone was watching her and had decided that she needed to pay for some imagined betrayal. What that betrayal could be, it was beyond her.

It was almost more than she could take.

The one comfort was that Gavin was there with her. His police car was fixed, and they were on their way back to LaMar Pond.

"When we get to your place, pack up a few

things. Enough to get you through a week, maybe. Then we'll get you to the safe house we have ready for you," he said.

"Fine. Whatever." She'd agree to anything if it meant catching this guy and protecting those around her. "Could we stop by my work, though? I keep a spare diabetic kit there. You know—tester and some glucagon shots. Just in case I need it."

"Sure thing. That's a reasonable request."

"Of course it is. I'm a reasonable person."

She lifted her chin, ignoring the snicker coming from the driver's side of the car. She had to force her lips not to smile, although they managed to twitch.

Twenty minutes later, Gavin parallel parked in front of the clinic. The window had been repaired. Someone had even rehung the Christmas lights. Between the snow and the decorations about the town, the whole scene looked like a picture on the box of a scenic puzzle. No one looking at the town would know of the menace that was among them.

"It doesn't look any different, does it?"

"Hmm?" Gavin turned off the engine and faced her, pocketing his key.

Alexa lifted a hand and made a waving motion to indicate the clinic. "Look at it, Gavin.

Noah was almost killed here. A sniper with a bone to pick with me shot out the window, and it looks like nothing has changed. Like the whole episode was just erased. Isn't that crazy? Someone gets shot, and the world keeps going."

Briefly, his warm hand covered hers. Her entire arm tingled. Then his hand was gone.

"Lexie, no one has forgotten. Trust me. Something like that tends to stay with you. But people have to go on."

"I know. I'm being silly, I guess." She slid her hand to the door handle. "Let's do this."

"It's not silly. And wait for me."

Alexa rolled her eyes, but she waited for him. He sauntered around the vehicle to get her door. Like a gentleman. She knew that it was more about scoping the scene for possible threats than being a gentleman, but it was nice nevertheless. When he was convinced it was safe, he opened the door for her to get out.

Glancing around, she saw that it was a busy day at the clinic. There was a multitude of cars and buggies in the parking lot.

"I wonder if they have a full staff today," she murmured.

Gavin shot her a look. "No."

"What?" She gave him her best innocent look. Judging from his glare, it wasn't that convincing.

"You know what. You can't work until the stalker is caught."

The moment she entered the clinic, a chorus of greetings met her ears. Within a minute, she was surrounded.

"Are you okay?" Megan caught her in a hug, holding on tight. The urge to cry swamped her. She hadn't realized how much she'd grown to like the other girl. She'd held herself aloof for so long. It was hard to remember the last time she was hugged by another person. It felt good. She hugged her back before stepping away.

"I'm good. Really. But I have to be off until things settle down." It was hard to speak around the lump in her throat.

Megan nodded, but her eyes were giving Gavin some serious attention. He didn't acknowledge her, his eyes sweeping the clinic. Feeling an unexpected surge of amusement, Alexa bit back a grin. He was well aware of the other girl, and it made him uncomfortable. She could see his cheeks flushing under Megan's stare.

Several of her Amish patients approached her, speaking in soft Pennsylvania Dutch, which in this area was mostly German flavored with their own dialectal changes, including a few English words sprinkled in. Alexa had taken five years of German, plus had studied in Germany for a year in college. Although she didn't understand everything, she understood more than enough to hold a conversation. While they normally spoke English in public, the Amish people she'd gotten to know knew she appreciated the opportunity to use her German skills.

Suddenly she realized that Gavin was waiting for her. Excusing herself, she walked through the door to the nurses' station. Megan approached her. "I'm glad you're here. Dr. Quinton is out now. He came down with the flu. He didn't even call in. Just sent an email. It must be pretty bad. That man never calls in sick, but it's okay. Some doctor from Erie came down as our replacement. He's nice enough." Megan lowered her voice. "He's kind of arrogant, though. Like he's better than us."

"Oh no! Who's the doctor?" Alexa asked.

"Dr. Jackson."

She heard Gavin's sharp intake of breath. Before she could turn to him, the new doctor came out into the waiting room. He was a handsome man. Dark hair. Blue eyes. And he bore a definite resemblance to Gavin. The doctor started to speak. His startled glance landed on Gavin. He paled, turned red and his words stuttered to a stop. Alexa guessed what was going on a split second before Gavin spoke, his tone brittle. Bitter.

"Sam."

The doctor straightened. He flashed a charming smile at the group, but even to a stranger like Alexa, it reeked of discomfort. "Gavin! How nice to see you. It's—"

"No time for a family reunion, Sam. Alexa is just here to collect her things. She's going to be out for a few days."

The doctor didn't like that; she could tell instantly. "Now see here, Gavin. I know you have a job to do, but so do I. This clinic is desperately short on nurses."

"That may be the case, Sam. I can't do anything about it, though. As long as she works here, the maniac after Lexie will continue to be a danger to the rest of the staff and your patients."

Megan caught Alexa's eye. *Lexie?* she mouthed. Alexa grimaced. Then she bit back a groan. Dr. Jackson was glaring at Gavin as if he was at fault for the whole situation. Gavin, she could see, was uncomfortable. He was still doing his best to remain professional about the matter.

Alexa couldn't believe this was happening. Her best course of action was to ignore them, get her stuff, and then she and Gavin could be on their way. She kept her spare diabetic kit and her favorite tea in the cupboard in the nurses' station. The locker that she'd been given smelled, and she hadn't been able to get odor out. Walking over to the cupboard where she kept her stuff, she turned the latch to open it.

A loud click came from inside the cupboard. Confused, she paused. Shrugging, she reached out to pull the cupboard open.

"No! Get away!" Gavin roared. He flew at her and brought her to the ground. Pain shot up her arm when her elbow slammed into the tile floor. He hovered over her, protectively, blocking the room from her view.

The cupboard that belonged to her exploded, taking the rest of the cupboards with it. Debris flew. Particleboard showered upon them in dust and small chunks.

Her personal cupboard had been rigged with a bomb. She got the message. This was personal. The man who was after her had said he'd punish her. That bomb had been put there just for her.

A sizzling sound erupted in the ensuing silence. Alexa smelled smoke. There was a fire somewhere.

Her stalker was determined to kill her. He didn't care how many lives he took in his attempts. He would never stop until she was dead.

Flames shot up the exploded particleboard cupboard. Leaping to his feet, Gavin grabbed the fire extinguisher from the wall and doused the rapidly expanding flames with the thick white foam. The flames hissed and sputtered, but gradually they were smothered and died out.

"Clear the place," he bellowed at receptionist. She jumped as if waking up and then ran from the room. He could hear the smoke alarm going off and the commotion of people being evacuated from the clinic.

He bent and scooped Alexa up in his arms, carrying her outside.

"Over here!" Megan was motioning to him from the parking lot. Still carrying Alexa, he moved that way. He deposited her in a sitting position on the hood of his cruiser.

"Lexie." Gavin scooted back from her, running his gaze up and down her from head to foot, checking to make sure she wasn't injured. He could hardly wrap his mind around what had happened. He'd been a cop for four years. In that time, he had seen some pretty bad stuff. But nothing had left him feeling as shaken as seeing that cupboard explode, knowing that Alexa had almost been blown up right in front of his eyes.

"Alexa, can you hear me?" Sam asked, standing on her other side. All sign of the spoiled older brother was gone. Now, Sam was in doctor mode.

She'd be in good hands. Sam might not have been his favorite person, but he was a competent doctor.

Gavin swiped a gentle hand down her hair, removing some dust and debris. When he saw the way his hand shook, he dropped it.

"I'm fine, guys. Stop hovering." Alexa pushed herself up off the car into a standing position.

It brought her face close to his. Too close. All he could think of, looking into her shocked blue eyes, was kissing her.

The moment that crossed his mind, he was horrified. No way did he just think about kissing her seconds after she avoided a bomb. But he had.

Gavin stepped back from her. Both to get some distance between him and the woman who was proving to be too distracting for his own good, and to survey the damage.

There were no flames on the outside of the building. Nor did he see any smoke. It looked like he might have extinguished all the fire inside. He used his radio to call the explosion in to the station. The clinic was now a crime scene. He also made sure to tell the dispatcher to send out someone from the bomb squad.

Sam was beside him. He hadn't seen his brother for several years now. He hadn't changed much. The arrogant swagger he'd been sporting a few minutes before the explosion had proved that. Still the entitled older son. The one who was important, and who expected everyone else to fall over backward to do what he wanted.

Which wouldn't have been bad if it had ended there. His brother's attitude he could ignore. What he couldn't ignore was what his brother had done to him, and in the end, what he had taken from him.

Now wasn't the time to think about the past. Gavin had a psychopath on his hands.

"Sam, for the safety of the employees and the patients here, you'll have to close the clinic for a few days. Until we have the perp in jail."

Gavin avoided his brother's eyes. In this instance, he was in charge. His brother had to listen. Gavin needed to protect the innocent from a vicious stalker spiraling out of control.

"Don't worry, Gavin. We'll close. As of right now."

Gavin relaxed his shoulders, allowing the tension to drain from them. He'd been prepared to do battle over this issue, but was glad he wouldn't have to.

He watched as the emergency crews—the fire department and the bomb squad—arrived. Then another police vehicle followed. Voices swelled around him as the people visiting the neighboring establishments saw that something big was happening at the clinic.

"Gavin—"

"I have a job to do, Sam." Gavin glanced at Alexa. Surely, he could leave her with Sam. His brother was married now, so Lexie wasn't in any danger from his charm and charisma.

He needn't have worried. His Lexie had no intention of being left behind. She ignored the doctor's outstretched arm and command to remain where she was and moved to Gavin's side.

That's when it hit him. Did he really just think of her as *his*? Yeah, that wasn't going to happen. He felt empty admitting that to himself. He'd been okay with being a perpetual bachelor. He'd had a job he was good at, friends he could trust and a life he was comfortable with. Any stray regrets had been pushed aside. Now, those regrets were pushing back, staring him in the face.

And the biggest regret was watching him with blue-gray eyes.

Eyes he could get used to seeing every single day.

What was wrong with him? He needed to focus.

"Gavin?"

He slanted a grin at her. "Stick with me."

"You got it."

He winked at her. When he saw Trevor Stone from the bomb squad talking to Parker and the chief, he walked over, aware of Alexa at his heels. Good. At this point, he definitely did not want to let the woman out of his sight. She was in too much danger. A man who went through the trouble of planting a bomb in her space wasn't going to quit. Gavin felt as if someone had reached in and tied his stomach in a large knot.

He could admit it to himself. He was falling fast for the pretty blonde. He knew he'd have to distance himself when this was over. But he'd never be able to live with himself if he let someone else take his place beside her and she got hurt. Or died. For whatever reason, she was his to protect. He would do so, no matter the cost.

He proceeded to greet the men. "Chief. Parker. Trevor. What do ya know?"

"Hey, Jackson." Trevor Stone ducked his head in acknowledgment as they approached. He pushed his glasses up on the bridge of his nose before answering. "This wasn't a professionally put together bomb. It's very amateurish work. It was triggered by the door of cupboard being opened. There don't seem to be any other bombs on the premises."

"No bombs," Parker broke in, his voice deadly serious, "but there is something you all need to see."

Which meant that Parker had found something. Something big. "Lead the way," Gavin said.

The small group walked silently back into the clinic. As they walked past where the cupboard had exploded, Gavin felt a hand gripping his sleeve. Without breaking stride, he reached his opposite hand over and covered Alexa's. When he released it, she didn't drop her hand from his arm. That was just fine with him. She could keep hold of him if it made her feel better. He didn't mind at all.

The group stopped when they reached the back room and stood before a row of lockers. They had been forced open, locks cut off.

One was standing open.

He heard Alexa's shocked intake of air.

"That's Dr. Quinton's locker!"

Gavin narrowed his eyes. "Was he scheduled to work this morning? Would he have been here when we were at the King place?"

"Normally yes." Alexa's gaze was glued to the locker. "Megan told me that he had sent in an email this morning. Said he had the flu."

Sure, he did. It was as good an excuse as any. With so many people out, no one would think to doubt him. And he'd be free to go on a shooting spree.

Her hand tightened its grip on him. Gavin reached back and looped an arm around her shoulders, hugging her lightly before stepping away from her. She let him go, and he approached the locker.

There was a stack of pictures lying inside the locker. The top one showed Lexie and Marvin at his farm. Marvin was sitting on a chair, while she stood close to his side. It might have looked intimate, but Gavin could see the blood pressure cuff on his arm.

Marvin's image had been crossed out with a black marker.

Reaching into his pocket, Gavin pulled out his gloves and slipped them on. Going to the locker, he picked up the stack of pictures. Each one showed Lexie in different poses. Some were taken here in the clinic. Some were taken at clients' homes.

Some were taken in her home.

His blood chilled when he came across a picture of Lexie sleeping on the couch. The rose was next to her. Moving to the next picture, he saw a picture of himself handing her a plate of food. Then a picture of her working with Noah. Again, Noah had been crossed out.

Suddenly he stopped. "Lexie, who's this?"

She moved quickly at the urgency in his voice. When she reached out to grab the picture, he pulled it back. "Don't touch it. It's evidence."

She leaned in closer. Her eyes widened and her face grew pale. "That's Eli Schwartz. I'm supposed to see him on Monday."

His face had been crossed out with an X.

"Change of plans. We're going out to see him today. Now."

It might already be too late.

NINE

She couldn't believe the stalker was Dr. Quinton. The man was gruff. He was irritable. He certainly didn't like it when he found her "socializing," as he put it, even when she was only being friendly to make a patient more comfortable.

But a killer?

That was one she'd never seen coming.

A thought struck her. "Gavin?"

"Yeah?" He broke off his conversation with the chief and looked at her.

"Sorry. Didn't mean to interrupt."

"No, that's okay. What's on your mind?"

All the officers were watching her intently. It made her uncomfortable, but what she had to say involved their investigation.

"The day that Noah was shot, I remember being surprised that Dr. Quinton didn't run up to see what the commotion was all about. I asked Megan where he'd been, and she said she'd seen him going into the back. I still thought he should have heard something. Come to investigate, you know what I mean?"

"Miss Grant," the chief interrupted. "I'm assuming that there's a back door to this establishment. Could he have gone out the door without triggering an alarm of some kind?"

"Oh. Yes, he certainly could have." It would certainly explain why he hadn't come to see what all the fuss was about.

"Lexie, when did you see Quinton that day? I seem to recall he got snarky with you," Gavin commented.

"That's right! When I received the flowers! He appeared as if he'd been working, but he came around the front of the reception desk. I have no idea where he came from."

"Chief, I want to go check up on Eli Schwartz. I think we should probably have an ambulance sent there just in case," Gavin said.

The chief nodded. The calm she'd seen before was replaced with an air of implacable determination. "Do that. I will have an ambulance sent that way. Parker, you follow after him." He glanced at his watch. "I know you two are off the clock—"

"I'm not leaving, sir. Not when we're this close."

The anxiety that had started to build when the chief had announced he should be off duty faded. The idea of facing this without Gavin at her side made her shudder. She knew she was a strong woman. She'd been through too much not to be. But this was something she had no experience with, no way to deal with on her own.

"Yes, sir. I'm not leaving now, either," Parker said, exchanging glances with Gavin. There was a true bond of friendship between these men. It was good that Gavin was surrounded by people who had his back.

She had only herself to rely on.

"I will start digging into the good doctor's background. See what we can find on him," Parker said.

"I'd be interested to see if he has any connection to Chicago," Gavin ground out.

"As would I," the chief murmured. "Gentlemen, let's get this man."

Gavin set the photos down, and took a picture with his cell phone of each one that had

Alexa and another person in it. Then he put the originals in a clear plastic bag and ran his fingers along the top to seal it. When he handed it to the chief, the men exchanged glances. They were all taking this very seriously. He tugged off his gloves and threw them away. Grabbing her hand, he pulled her out of the clinic.

"You coming, Parker?" he shouted over his shoulder.

"Right behind you."

He held the door to his cruiser open for her. No flourishes or grins this time. She missed his playfulness. He loped around to his door while she buckled herself in.

"Where's Eli's place?" He opened the computer settled on the swinging arm that extended from his dashboard, and called up the GPS. When Alexa gave him the address, he punched it in, then gave it to Parker. "In case we get separated."

She nodded, suddenly feeling her eyes sting. It was common enough for patients to have a delayed reaction to a shocking event. She hadn't expected to experience it herself.

"Lexie."

She jerked her head up at her name. By his

tone of voice, she'd guess Gavin had said her name more than once.

"Sorry. I was in my own world for a moment."

"It's all right. There's a small case under the seat. Pull it out." She did as he said. Inside, there was a small, weathered-looking Bible. She raised a questioning brow at him. This wasn't the time to have a Bible lesson. He shifted the car into gear and started driving. "That's my uncle's Bible. I keep it with me. I sometimes read it on my lunch break. Anyway, when he died, I kept it. I have a passage bookmarked. Open it."

Deciding to play along, she did as he asked. Not only was the page bookmarked, but he had highlighted a verse. Curious, she kept the bookmark in place and flipped through the Bible. There were other verses highlighted throughout the pages. Obviously, these were verses that meant something to him.

"Do me a favor. Read the one I have highlighted."

She cleared her throat. "Umm, read it to myself or out loud?"

"Out loud, if you will."

Reading out loud always made her feel ridiculous. She shrugged. The man had saved her life. The least she could do would be to read something to him. "'And God shall wipe away all tears from their eyes; and there shall be no more death, neither sorrow, nor crying, neither shall there be any more pain: for the former things are passed away.'"

Wow. Sounded good to her.

"That's Revelation 21:4."

"But I don't see this happening. I mean, there's still pain. And death. Horrible things are happening every day. Even here, in LaMar Pond. I came here to get away from these things. But it followed me." She flushed, embarrassed by her outburst. But it was true. Where was God in all that?

"Lexie, let me tell you something." He started, then stopped. Whatever it was, it wasn't something he enjoyed talking about. His eyes tightened. She heard him swallow.

"Gavin, don't feel you have to—"

He waved at her, silencing her protests. "I do have to. When Uncle Leo gave me a place to live, he gave me more than that. He gave me purpose and value. And he opened my eyes to faith. Something that he would want me to pass on."

The GPS signaled a turn coming up. Gavin completed the turn in silence. Then he began speaking again. "Growing up, it was just me and Sam with my parents. You'd think we'd be close, right? He was only two years older than me. And for most of my life, I really looked up to him." He made a scoffing sound. "Who wouldn't? Sam was brilliant. Everything he did, he succeeded at. He decided when he was in like eighth grade that he was going to be a doctor. My parents decided to start saving for his medical school. Everything they could spare. Do you know what they saved toward my college?"

Her heart ached at the pain that layered beneath his smooth voice.

"Nothing. Now, I wasn't a star student. I got average grades. But I always expected to go to college. When I told them I was looking into them, they looked at me, and I could see the guilt in their eyes. That's when it hit me. For years they'd asked Sam about his college plans. They'd talked about the money they were saving up. For him. When I asked them, they had nothing to say. You know why? They had made no plans for my future. Because they hadn't expected anything from me."

That had to have hurt.

"Maybe, they meant to—"

He laughed. "You're so sweet. Lexie. You always want to heal everyone, don't you? I admire that about you. You tend to put others first. Like how you put your patients' needs above your own safety. But no. They flat-out told me that they didn't expect me to do anything amazing with my life. I'd always known that I was second best. Parker, he knows some of this. He had a problem with his dad for a while 'cause his dad was disappointed in his wanting to be a cop. Thought he could do better. Mine? They didn't have any expectations for me at all."

"Gavin, I wish I knew what to say."

He shrugged. "So I got a job, and some loans, and I went to college as a political science major. There I met Lacey." His voice grew remote. "She and I were inseparable. When we got engaged, I couldn't wait to show her off. She came home with me on Thanksgiving weekend. At Christmas, I found out she'd been sneaking around with my brother. I broke the engagement. If that wasn't bad enough, though, my parents didn't care. They just said that she wasn't right for me. My brother couldn't see that what he did was wrong. I moved in with Uncle Leo. He, at least, always thought I could do something with my life. When I went to the police academy and graduated, he was prouder of me than anyone had ever been. My parents? They didn't even bother to show up."

Wow. That was so sad. She tried to swallow past the lump in her throat.

"I was angry at first. But then, I began to learn about his faith."

He halted at a stop sign. "Lexie, that faith has gotten me through some pretty tough times. It's given me a purpose. I know that here on earth I might not be the best at anything. But God loves me anyway. He loves me, and someday all the pain, all the anguish will be gone. That's my hope."

They arrived at the Schwartz residence. She bent to replace the Bible. He stopped the car, then stilled her hand with his. "Keep it. I'm giving it to you. You might need it. I think that you could use the hope that Bible has given me when things were tough."

His face was grim. She looked up. The front door was wide open.

"Don't get out yet," Gavin told Alexa, his senses on high alert. "Let's wait for Parker. I don't want to go inside without backup. Not when we have no idea what we're going to find."

Five minutes later, Parker pulled in behind him.

"Stay here," Gavin ordered. Then he saw Alexa's face. It was pale and distressed; her eyes were wide. He had a feeling she was blaming herself. He'd do anything to erase that fear from her mind. "Please, Lexie. I need you to be safe."

She glanced his way. Her tear-drenched eyes struck him right in the chest. She didn't let those tears fall, though. Blinking fast, she sat up straight and set her jaw.

What a woman. His admiration for her grew.

"I'll wait here. But don't you go getting yourself shot, you hear me, Gavin Jackson? I'll not have you hurt on my account."

He couldn't help it. He leaned over the console area and kissed her cheek. Those blue-gray eyes blinked at him, shocked. "I'll be careful. I need to lock the doors. Do me a favor and get down."

That way he wouldn't worry about her being hit by stray bullets.

Before he could do anything else dumb, he bolted from the car. He had kissed her! That was not his smartest move to date, but even while he chastised himself, he couldn't regret it. She was a very special lady. He might not have a future with her, but he would always have a special place for her in his heart.

Parker's boots made muffled stomping noises as he came up next to him. Wordlessly the two grim men headed toward the house. At the base of the steps, Parker stopped.

"I'll watch out here. Cover your back."

Gavin nodded. Parker had a clear view of both the doorway and his car. Peering back, he couldn't see Lexie inside. Good. She'd gotten down. One less thing to worry about.

Slowly, keeping his service weapon out and his eyes constantly sweeping the area around him, Gavin moved up the steps. Entering the doorway, he halted, listening. Nothing. Cautiously, he continued into the house, entering the kitchen. The house had an open floor plan. From where he stood, he could plainly see Eli Schwartz lying on the floor. The man looked about his own age, maybe a little older.

He was too late.

Moving to the body, he reached down to feel the side of Eli's neck. To his surprise, there was a pulse. It was faint, but the man was alive. Barely. It was a good thing there was an ambulance on the way. If they got here within the next few minutes, they might be able to save him.

Whoever this stalker was, he wasn't a very good shot. Which was fortunate for the men he'd gone after.

And for him and Lexie, he thought, recalling dodging bullets the previous day.

What about Brett's death? If it was the same perp, he'd had no trouble killing the man Lexie had been engaged to. But that was in a hospital and only involved switching the man's medication. Just another piece of the evidence piling up against Dr. Quinton.

Gavin heard a shuffling sound above him. He walked upstairs and found a door jammed shut. Removing the chair blocking it, he opened the door slowly. The woman lying on the floor had to have been Eli's wife. She was alive; her pulse was strong. She had a large bump on her temple. The stalker hadn't bothered trying to kill her but had only knocked her out. She'd have a nasty headache when she came to. She moved again, and her foot jostled a chair. That was the sound he'd heard.

Using his radio, Gavin called in the attack on the couple.

Stomping feet on the stairs brought him racing from the room. He skidded to a stop when he heard the familiar voices. The ambulance had arrived. "Hey guys, I have another patient up here."

One of the paramedics stepped into view at the bottom of the steps. "I'm on it."

Gavin left them to do their job while he searched the house, room by room. It didn't come as any surprise to him that he found no sign of Quinton anywhere. The man had probably left long before Gavin entered the house.

A few minutes later, another complication arose when the Schwartz children arrived home. It was late Friday afternoon. The Amish school had let out.

He did his best to calm the children. There were five of them. The oldest was a teenager, and the youngest was about nine or ten. They were confused and scared.

He was a bit out of his element. Except for the kids of his fellow officers, he didn't have much experience with children. They made him feel awkward, but he did envy his colleagues who were fathers.

Before he could get too flustered, though, Alexa entered the room. Parker followed her.

"I'm going to search the property line, as long as she's with you," Parker said, then ducked out again.

Alexa, it turned out, was good with children. It seemed to help that these particular kids were familiar with her. "The ambulance is going to take your father to the hospital."

The oldest child, a boy, threw a wary glance

at Gavin, then quietly asked her a question in Pennsylvania Dutch. She responded in a soft, reassuring voice, speaking in German. He'd forgotten that she said she spoke the language.

"Ma'am, you might want to reconsider—"

Gavin, Alexa and the children looked over at the paramedic talking to a woman, Eli's wife, who was walking down the steps. She was walking with care, and her eyes were squinting, probably from the pain. But she didn't slow down.

"*Nee*. I am not going on your ambulance. I should be with my children."

"Waneta, can I do anything for you?" Alexa stepped forward.

The woman's face creased in a small smile. "Ah, Alexa, *denke*. *Nee*, I am fine. My Eli is going to the hospital."

Alexa's face grew tense. "I know. I'm sorry, Waneta. Someone is following me. He's going after some of my patients."

The woman's gaze sharpened. "This man, the police will get him."

"Yes, ma'am, we will," Gavin stated. He wouldn't give up until they did.

"*Gut*." She turned her brown eyes back to Alexa. "*Gott* will help us. He will help you."

Alexa didn't respond to that. She seemed

to be getting the God talk everywhere they went. First Naomi. Then him. Now Waneta. He didn't know how she had felt about his attempt at witnessing in the car. He might not have been the best witness. He wouldn't second-guess that, though. God had put him there at that moment. He'd have to trust.

"Mrs. Schwartz, I know you said you didn't want to go to the hospital for treatment, but can we get a driver to take you there to be with your husband?" Gavin asked.

She considered for a moment. "*Jah.* That would work. My *kinder* can go and stay with my sister."

At least he could count that as one family out of harm's way.

Eli, Marvin and Noah would all be kept under guard in the hospital. He sent a text to Chief Kennedy to update him.

Quinton's picture had been released to the surrounding precincts. By morning, it would be in the papers, too. Letting the public and those in charge know to keep a lookout.

Noah Hostetler would be released from the hospital in the morning. He and his wife Naomi agreed to go stay with another family.

Marvin King's sister Linda had not been found yet. They'd continue the search tomorrow.

After leaving the Schwartz place, Gavin drove Lexie to her residence. After searching for threats, he paced her living room while she packed for the safe house.

"What about Cinnamon?" she asked. "The police station is no place for a cat."

She was worried about the cat. Part of him found that amusing, but at the same time, he wanted to roll his eyes. Still, it was endearing. "He's okay. I had the chief grab Cinnamon and my cat, Whiskers. They've been at his house most of the day. His kids are overjoyed at the prospect of caring for the cats. The chief's going to keep them at his house until this is done. Who knows how long it will be until we'll be back in our homes to care for them."

She bit her lip. The corners of her mouth still turned up. She was fighting a smile.

"What?"

She gave up and laughed. He smiled in reflex. "I can't imagine you naming a cat Whiskers."

He chuckled. "It was the first thing that came to mind. I mean, what do you name a cat?"

They headed out and grabbed something to eat at a drive-through. He placed the bag containing his sandwich on the back floorboard.

He'd eat when they got to the house he was taking her to. He noticed that she was reluctant to open her salad with chicken. Even though her stomach was growling.

"Eat, honey. I can wait. But I don't mind if you eat now. I know you're hungry."

Honey? Since when did he call a woman honey? It just slipped out. Gauging by her wide eyes, she'd noticed it, too. But the soft smile she sent his way made his pulse race.

He needed to find a way to stop this growing attraction between them. She deserved someone better than him. When he let his emotions take over, it was never good.

She opened her chopped salad and took a bite. He could tell that she wasn't in the mood to eat. She swallowed a sip of water, then turned her attention to him. "Tell me about your uncle."

Ah, she'd just handed him the means to warn her away from him. He sighed. It had to be done, but he wished with all his might that it didn't. If only.

"Uncle Leo was a great guy. Funny. Loyal. A good, solid cop." He took a sip of his Diet Coke. Here was the hard part. "As you know, he also had diabetes. Despite what his doctor had told him to do, he didn't take care of himself. That was my job. And I failed at it."

She paused, the fork halfway to her mouth. "Failed? How?"

"I had just gotten word from my mom that my brother and Lacey were getting married. She couldn't understand why I wasn't happy for them. Imagine that? Me being upset that my fiancée was going to marry my brother. According to my mom, he was the better fit for a girl like Lacey." Sam was a better everything, he thought, the familiar bitterness rising inside. "I went to the gym to work off some of my anger. In my irritation, I purposely left my phone in my car. I didn't want her calling me again. Well, she didn't call me. But Leo did. Twice. His sugar levels had gotten very low and bottomed out. By the time I got to him, he'd gone into a diabetic coma. He never came out of it. If I'd gotten there sooner, I might have been able to help." He paused. Better just say it.

"I'm not good with relationships, Lexie. I get stubborn, and I let people down. Lacey apparently knew that. My mom knew that. And Leo died because of it."

TEN

Alexa had no idea what to say to him. She had thought about Gavin's story all evening. She'd even tried to talk with him a time or two about it. To no avail. Gavin had decided to shut her out. Why? Because of his feeling that he'd let his uncle die.

When he'd left the safe house around eight, she was exhausted. She tried to listen as Claire Zerosky chattered to her, but in the end, begged off early, claiming she had a headache.

It wasn't a lie. But her heart hurt as much, if not more, than her head. She had understood what Gavin was telling her in the car. He was letting her know that once the case was solved and her stalker was caught, he would be out of her life. Just like her father, who'd abandoned her so many years ago. Just like her mother or her brother. Even Brett, the man she'd thought she'd grow old with, was gone.

It didn't matter. It was just one more sign that she was right. People left her. Maybe not by choice. Maybe there were extenuating circumstances, but it didn't change the outcome. No one stayed for her.

Well, at least Gavin had let her know they had no future. Now all she needed to do was figure out how to keep herself from falling the rest of the way for a man who had no intention of sticking around.

At around five in the morning, she gave up trying to sleep and went downstairs. Gavin wasn't there yet, but Claire was up. Alexa gave her a smile and went into the kitchen to fix breakfast.

"You want something, Claire?" she called out to the other woman.

"Nah. It's too early to eat. I just made some coffee, though. Help yourself."

Alexa loved the aroma of coffee, but hadn't learned to like the bitter taste. And with her diabetes, she couldn't add enough creamer to make it palatable without making her blood sugar go crazy. She stuck with water and tea.

She brought her omelet to the table to eat it. Her eyes fell on the Bible that Gavin had insisted she take. She hadn't wanted to, but now, she had to admit to being curious. Slowly she began to leaf through it as she ate. Some of the passages were unclear. She decided that she really liked some of the books in the New Testament. Not that she was a believer yet. It would take more reading and study, but she was interested enough to do that. It might need to wait until the current situation was resolved.

Gavin arrived at eight. He strolled in looking like he hadn't had any more sleep than she had. His greeting, however, was casual. He wasn't letting on that anything had bothered him.

"Hey, there, Zee, Alexa. What do ya know?"

Alexa. Not Lexie. She hadn't realized how much she liked hearing the nickname in his deep voice.

"Hey, Jackson. You're early." Claire stood and stretched. "I wasn't expecting you until ten."

From where she sat, Alexa could see the tide of red sweeping up the back of his neck. Suddenly she wondered if he'd come to check on her. That might mean that she was getting to him, as well. He was just too stubborn to admit it. Which might not make a difference.

She reminded herself to be careful and not read anything into his actions. Sure, he was a great guy. Gavin was honorable, fun and made her pulse race. He was also, however, a man who had made it very clear that he was not in the market for a relationship. Any feelings that developed were going to be one sided, and she could not put her heart in that kind of risk again. It would destroy her.

"What's going on?" she asked, more to hide her jumbled emotions than any other reason.

"What's going on," he replied, "is that we are going to start going to your Amish patients' homes today and warn them about your stalker. The ones that Lieutenants Tucker and Willis couldn't reach yesterday. There are only a few of them. It shouldn't take us too long."

Oh, great. A day in the car with the man who'd let her know in no uncertain terms that they had no future.

At first, it was awkward. Soon, however, their joint mission of warning her patients outweighed feelings of awkwardness. They were still on the search for a man who wanted her dead, a man who seemed to feel he had the right to kill anyone who got too close to her. Which also made Gavin a target.

"I'd already figured that out." He shrugged when she mentioned it to him.

"I can't understand why he'd do this, though."

Gavin rubbed the back of his neck. "I don't know what to tell you, Lexie."

Ah, he'd slipped and called her Lexie again. She really liked it when he called her that in his deep voice. It was a small thing, but it made her happy to hear it.

He passed an Amish buggy on the street. Craning her neck, she peered at the family inside the buggy. A young couple, maybe about twenty. No one she knew. "Stalkers don't usually make much sense. They are driven by extremes. Obsessed. To people around them, they might appear perfectly normal," Gavin said and glanced her way briefly.

She watched the scenery flash by. "I get that. But, Gavin, he's a doctor. He knows that the men I work with are only patients. That's what I don't get. Why would he get jealous of them?"

They pulled into the first house. The hustle and bustle of a family working paused temporarily as a police car drove up the lane. It wasn't a usual occurrence to see cops at an Amish house. When Alexa stepped from the vehicle, several of the children came running, telling her about the news.

"Alexa! We have new sisters! *Zwillingbopplin!*"

"Twins," she murmured to Gavin.

Levi, the father, stepped out on the porch.

Levi was a popular Amish name in the district, she knew. The people in the area referred to him as Painter Levi, to differentiate him from some of the others. She'd always liked the pleasant man. He was a good provider for his family and devoted to his wife and children.

"Nurse," he said, questioning her, "Lovina does not expect you today."

"I know that, Levi. I have come for something else. Can we talk? It's important."

Frowning, the man stepped aside so they could enter his residence. The house was spotless. The eldest daughter was stirring a pot on the stove. When she put down the wooden spoon, her father asked her softly to go upstairs and check on her mother and new sisters.

Silently she left the room.

Once she'd gone, Gavin explained the reason for their presence at the house.

"I was never a patient of Nurse Grant," Levi protested. "She came to see my wife."

"That might be the case, sir, but someone has been watching Alexa, Nurse Grant. We have pictures. There's one of you with her at the door."

"You'd given me the cookies that Miriam, your daughter, had made for me as I was leaving," Alexa interjected.

The man's eyes brightened with memory. "*Jah!* Last month."

His face darkened. "You think someone will try to hurt me, or my family?"

Alexa winced. "It's a possibility. Can I show you a picture of the man who's stalking me? That way you can keep an eye out."

Levi agreed. Gavin fished his phone out of his pocket and searched through the pictures to find the one he was looking for. Alexa had seen it before, so she knew what Levi was looking at.

"We will watch for this man," Levi stated.

They left the house, promising to let the family know when there were any new developments.

Had they done any good? Sure, the family knew who to look for, but how would they protect themselves if danger came for them? They wouldn't use guns or violence against another person.

As Gavin drove along, Alexa felt herself tense. The family at the first house was safe. What would they find at the next house? Were they walking into a trap?

If Lexie got any tenser, she'd shatter.

Despite his resolution to keep his distance,

Gavin reached over and caught her hand in his before he could second-guess himself.

"Lexie, it could have been worse."

She huffed a loud sigh. He hid a smile. It wasn't funny. He knew she was frustrated, but she was cute. He fought the urge to brush his fingers down her cheek. Why did he always want to touch her? It wasn't like him. He had never been a demonstrative man.

"It's not just that. I hate this situation. I feel like I can never quite catch a break."

He frowned. "I know that your fiancé died. It was awful what happened to him. And the current situation is no picnic, but surely, once this is done, things will get better. Normal."

She leaned her head back against her seat and closed her eyes. When she laughed, he cringed a bit. The laugh was a harsh sound. A sad one. Not the way a laugh should sound. He found himself wishing he had the power to make her laugh from joy. Not that sad, hopeless noise.

She stopped laughing. "I don't know if I'd know what normal was. Gavin, my life has never been normal. Or happy. When I was a kid, my dad left. Just left. Got himself a brand-new family and forgot about his old one. My mom, she was an alcoholic. She had tried to straighten herself out, but after he left, she gave up. She drank herself to death. Neither my brother nor myself were enough of a reason to stop. After she died, I had nowhere to go. My brother is much older than me. He offered to let me come and stay with them. I knew he and his wife didn't really want me around."

Gavin felt a moment of guilt. At least he'd had Leo. And his parents loved him. They were just very uninvolved in his life.

"I know he died, but you had Brett."

She was already shaking her head. "You know what? I think Brett and I got together because we both had no one. We were friends, and we sort of drifted into being a couple. I don't know if we could have made it as a married couple. In the end, he died and left, just like everyone else."

What was he supposed to say to that?

"Lexie—"

"I'm sorry. I know you want to help, but I really don't want to discuss this anymore. Can we change the subject?"

He wanted to pursue it. For the first time, he wanted to be able to act on his emotions and tell a girl he had feelings for her. He'd never really been able to fully express himself, even with Lacey. But he couldn't. He didn't have the right to tell her about the feelings he was developing for her. He knew that it would be harder for her when they went their separate ways. Her story had made him see it more clearly than ever. She needed someone who would stay and put her first. Not a man who might be called away at a moment's notice. Certainly not a man who risked his life every day while performing his duties.

The next two houses they visited proved to be similar to the first. The Amish patients hadn't been harmed. There was that, at least. One man did report that his dog had chased someone away the night before. When he'd heard what was going on, he'd agreed to watch out.

At least neither he nor his family had been harmed.

Yet.

The quicker they found Quinton, the better off everyone would be.

Gavin's phone rang. He punched a button, putting it on speaker. "Jackson here. You're on speaker."

Hopefully, whoever was on the other end would be cool with Lexie hearing the conversation. Otherwise, he'd need to pull over and take the call. These roads were too slippery for him to drive and talk at the same time.

The person on the other end paused. "Hey, Jackson. It's Dan."

Lieutenant Dan Willis. "Yeah?"

"We have hit a snag with the investigation. We did some searching. We can't find any connection with Dr. Quinton and Chicago. But that doesn't seem to mean anything. Apparently, Dr. Quinton didn't exist until a couple of years ago."

"Didn't exist? He has a driver's license."

"Yes. But all the info on it is falsified. He didn't exist."

Gavin let the news sink in for a moment. "Witness Protection?"

"Who knows. Nothing concrete yet. We might need to actually send someone out to Chicago. The chief's waiting to hear back from the PD first."

If they needed someone to go there, he might convince the chief to let him go with Lexie. It would get her out of the way, and it would help him to find the links in the case. He hated the gaps in the investigation. It was making him nuts.

He disconnected with the lieutenant.

"It would make sense in an odd sort of way if he didn't exist."

He glanced at Lexie, furrowing his brow in confusion. "Run that by me again? How does it make sense?"

"Another doctor started the clinic a couple of years ago. Quinton came on staff later, not long after I arrived. The clinic is mostly funded by donations. And the doctors both poured their own resources into it. The clinic, while it will serve anyone, was set up primarily to service the Amish and Mennonite communities. If Quinton had to practice medicine with anonymity, that makes as much sense as anything else."

"So, we have checked in with all the patients in the pictures. The good news is that no one else has been attacked."

She shifted in her seat so that she was facing him. "The bad news is that they are still vulnerable."

"Yeah, maybe—"

He bit off the word as a white full-sized pickup truck roared up behind them. The vehicle inched forward. They were on a long stretch of country road. There wasn't much traffic. Why didn't he just pass if he was in such a hurry?

"Idiot," Gavin muttered. "Just because you're bigger, doesn't mean I can't give you a ticket."

He flipped on his lights and siren. Just a short blast to warn the guy off. It didn't work. Instead, the driver moved closer. This wasn't a careless driver. This was a man trying to run them down.

"Hold on, Lexie!" Gavin sped up, but there wasn't much he could do with the icy roads. Jabbing his radio, he waited for the dispatcher's voice to come on.

"Elise, it's Jackson. I'm on Route 89. Someone in a pickup truck is trying to run me off the road."

The truck slammed into his bumper. His cruiser fishtailed. He steered the wheels into the swerve, straightening his vehicle. In his rearview mirror, he could see a man wearing a dark hood. His features were in shadows. Quinton?

"What kind of car does the doctor drive?" he yelled across to Lexie. The truck was coming for them again. He pushed down on the accelerator, hoping to keep some distance between them.

Lexie was scooched down in her seat, hands braced against the dashboard. "That's his truck," she replied, voice tight. "I'd know it anywhere. See the red streak on the fender? A red truck backed into him three months ago."

"Elise, I have a confirmation. The truck belongs to our suspect. I believe him to be armed and very dangerous."

"Hold tight, Jackson. Backup is en route to intercept."

Hold tight. That would be easier if the road weren't so slippery. A sharp curve was directly in front. "Lord, please, help us make this curve."

"Amen," Lexie muttered beside him. It was the second prayer she'd said in her life.

They sailed around the corner, swerving. He felt the vehicle skidding out of control and held his breath. When the car straightened, he let his breath out and risked a look out the rearview window. He sucked in his breath again.

"Stay down!" he commanded Lexie. She slid lower in her seat, her terrified eyes fastened on his face. "He's got a gun!"

Fortunately, the driver seemed to be having trouble keeping the truck in control at the high speeds. Flashing lights were coming from ahead of them. Backup was on its way. The truck slowed then did a very dangerous three-point turn in the middle of the state highway.

It sped off in the opposite direction, spinning down the first road it past.

Turning the wheel with both hands, Gavin pulled over to the soft shoulder to recover his composure and to allow the other police cars room to maneuver.

The first cruiser zoomed past in pursuit of the truck. He recognized Miles Olsen at the wheel. He watched the sergeant's cruiser turn down the road after the truck and disappear. In his mind he whispered a prayer for his colleague. The second cruiser pulled directly in front of their position, facing the wrong way.

Claire Zerosky hopped out of the car, her short red hair flapping as she strode urgently to the driver's window. He rolled the window down at her approach.

"Y'all doing all right in there? Anyone hurt?"

He read the real concern in her eyes. He'd never take the friends he'd made on the LaMar Pond PD for granted again.

"I'm good. Lexie?" He turned his gaze on her, scanning for any injuries. They'd taken those turns pretty hard. He didn't think she'd been banged around too badly, but he wasn't taking chances.

"I'm good. Glad to see you, Claire." The smile she flashed at the other woman was warm.

Sergeant Zerosky laughed. The urgency rolled away from her. "You guys gave me a scare."

The radio crackled as Olsen spoke. "I found the truck. The vehicle had crashed on Burgundy Road. The suspect has fled the scene. I'm in pursuit. I repeat, the suspect is on foot, and he's armed."

Dr. Quinton was on the loose.

ELEVEN

Despite all their efforts, Dr. Quinton had not been found. Noah Hostetler had been released from the hospital. He and his family had left the same day to stay with another family. Alexa was relieved to know that they, at least, would be out of danger.

"If I have to stay in this house too much longer, I'm going to lose my mind." She moved her piece, the thimble, around the Monopoly board. And groaned as she landed on Park Place, which Claire owned.

The sergeant smirked. "Maybe not crazy, but if you keep playing this way, you'll be out of money."

"It's fake money, so it doesn't count," Alexa grumbled. She cast her eyes toward the windows. It was snowing again. Next week was Christmas. She'd not paid too much attention to the holiday in the past. It just seemed more of a commercial thing than a spiritual one. But since she'd been reading the Bible that had belonged to Gavin's uncle, she was starting to change her mind. She especially liked how both he and Gavin had made notes in the margins. It had never occurred to her before that people could make connections with the book. When this was all over, she was going to give the Bible back to Gavin, and she was going to get her own. Then she could start making her own connections and notes. Besides, she knew that the Bible was something he had cherished.

The front door burst open. She jumped, screeching. When Gavin strode into the room, she wilted back in her chair, glaring at him.

"Did you have to do that? You startled me. I thought for sure we'd been found."

Her pulse thudded in her veins. Not all because she was startled, though. She was chagrined by how happy she was to see him. He hadn't stopped by at all, the day before. Nor had she talked to him. Instead, he'd called and talked with Claire then hung up. Claire, however, made sure to relay to Alexa that he had specifically asked about Alexa. Several times.

My, it was good to see him. She had missed him yesterday. She liked the other officers, but she was growing very fond of Gavin's presence. Too fond.

Claire smiled and started to clear up the board.

Gavin cocked his head at his colleague, eyebrow raised. "I told Claire I'd be here today."

She shot her glare toward the redhead.

"You said you *might* stop by. I wasn't going to get Alexa's hopes up and then have you bail on us."

Alexa flushed. Was she that obvious?

"So Gavin," she said, flashing him her best innocent smile, "what do you know?"

He chuckled when he heard his own phrase turned back on him. "That's my line. But I'll answer. What I know is that we are out of here. The chief wants us to head to the hospital in Chicago to see what we can find about Dr. Quinton."

She stood and moved to the window. It would be nice to get out. But she didn't understand. "I thought you said he was in Witness Protection."

"That was a theory we floated, but it didn't check out. He wasn't being protected by any government agency. Which is why we need to go to see what he was into. And I told the chief you could be useful in the interview."

She wasn't so sure. She didn't like the thought of going into her old hospital again where people she'd worked with had turned on her. She'd been the recipient of too much gossip and malicious whispers to want to go back. Still, she would do it if it helped catch Quinton.

And if it would get her out of the safe house. "Sold."

She made it out to the car in record time. Gavin wasn't driving his cruiser today. Instead, he was driving a pickup truck that had seen better days. But it was meticulously clean. She so wasn't surprised. He was, however, wearing his police uniform. Which made sense. He was going on police business.

Then they drove into the airport. He grabbed a backpack from the truck and they headed in. The plane was already boarding. They sat in their seats. That's when what she was doing hit her. She was on a plane.

She. Was. On. A. Plane.

"Lexie? You okay?" Gavin leaned in so close, she could feel his breath on her face. Even that couldn't distract her from her present crisis.

"Um, no. Maybe I should have mentioned this before. But I have a serious fear of flying."

He took her hand. "It's going to be fine. You

know, planes are safer than cars. Your chances of dying on a plane—"

"Gavin!" she said through clenched teeth. "That is so not helpful."

They took off a few minutes later, and she squished her eyes closed as tightly as she could. The plane lurched a few times. Was it tipping? Her eyes flew open.

She became aware that Gavin was stroking her hand and wrist.

"It's fine, Lexie. It's just the plane setting its course. No worries."

Breathe. She needed to breathe and relax. This was going to be fine. In an hour and a half, they'd be in Chicago. She'd worry about the trip back when she got to that point.

Twenty minutes later, she hit another moment of panic. Her stomach grumbled. She'd been so busy worrying about getting ready to go with Gavin, she'd neglected to eat her mid-morning snack. She knew better than that, but time got away from her.

She looked at Gavin, panicked. He was calmly searching through his backpack. Reaching in deep, he brought out a plastic bag with an apple, a wedge of cheese and an ice pack. She stared in wonder. This man knew her so well. Even Brett rarely thought of her needs as a person with diabetes.

Thanking him, she reached for the bag from his hand. Electricity shot up her arm as their fingers met. Grabbing the bag, she moved her arm back from his. She took a bite of the apple, discreetly peeking up at him through her lashes. He was calmly watching the skyline out the window. Irritated, she crunched loudly on her apple. He obviously wasn't as affected by her as she was by him.

Another spot of rough turbulence hit.

Whatever happened, she hoped she wouldn't embarrass herself in front of Gavin by passing out. She didn't know if she'd ever be able to live something like that down.

The flight attendant came by with their snacks a few minutes later. The young man across from her tore into his bag of peanuts and popped an entire handful of them into his mouth.

The girl sitting beside him next to the window said something to him, and he began to laugh.

Alexa watched as he gasped. Then his hands went to his throat. Peanuts dribbled from his mouth. He continued to make the universal sign for choking.

"Peter?" the girl said. Then she began to shriek. "Peter! Someone help me!"

Alexa was already unbuckled and rising from her seat.

"Ma'am, please remain—"

"I'm a nurse," Alexa said briskly, brushing past the flight attendant. "That man's choking."

She was aware of Gavin standing beside her.

"Gavin, I need to get him standing, and I need him balanced so I can help him."

Squatting down next to the man, she stared into his panicked eyes. Her own panic had disappeared in the face of his distress. "Sir, I'm a nurse. Are you choking?"

He nodded.

"Okay. I'm going to help you, okay?"

Again, the man nodded. She could hear a slight rasp. Some air was getting through.

"Gavin, help me get him into a standing position. I need you to keep him from falling over." She commanded him, her whole attention focused on the man in need. On some level, she was aware that the other passengers were watching them. She couldn't worry about them. The young man's color was gone. Soon, he might pass out.

Without a word, Gavin helped the man to

stand. He braced his legs on the sides of the narrow aisle and held the man steady while Alexa slipped behind the man and efficiently brought her arms around the choking patient and placed the thumb of her left fist against his diaphragm. Moving her other hand on top of the first, she jerked them in and up. On the third attempt, a peanut shot from the man's mouth, and he wilted.

Gavin caught him before he could knock Alexa off her feet. Together, they eased the man back into his seat.

Alexa was pleased to note that his color was returning to his face. He was breathing freely, although there was still a harsh sound to it.

"Is he going to be fine?"

Alexa turned to see the flight attendants were hovering near her. The one she'd shoved her way past earlier was looking at her with concerned eyes.

"Yes," Alexa told her.

The man's girlfriend started to sob. "Thank you so much! He would have died if you and your boyfriend hadn't been here to help."

Alexa felt a fierce blush burn her cheeks. She didn't dare turn to look at Gavin. They thought he was her boyfriend? He must hate that.

She mentally shrugged. That didn't matter

at the moment. She turned to the man the girl had called Peter.

"Peter," she said. The man opened his eyes. "I am going to ask you to see a doctor once we land, even though you are not choking anymore. Just as a precaution to make sure you didn't do any damage."

"We'll call the paramedics at the airport," one of the flight attendants promised. "They can have him checked out as soon as we arrive in Chicago."

Emergency over, Alexa and Gavin returned to their seats. Awkwardness set in as she tried to ignore the numerous glances that kept being sent her way. She grimaced when she realized that someone was aiming a phone her way.

Ugh. Just what she needed. Her face posted on social media. She turned her head away to avoid the camera.

Her gaze met Gavin's. She blinked at the admiration in his eyes.

He leaned toward her. "You are amazing."

She blushed, ducking her head. Still, she couldn't help the small thrill that went through her at his words. She'd never had anyone tell her she was amazing before.

Her smile faded. He might think she was amazing. But that didn't mean he was going to stay.

* * *

Gavin couldn't believe the calm woman beside him was the same woman who'd been so afraid of flying. Her cheeks were a little red, but he rather thought that was due to all the people straining their necks to see her. The woman who had saved a man's life on a plane.

He'd told her she was amazing, and she was. How else would one describe a woman who had put aside her own fear in order to save a life, and then sat back down like she hadn't done anything remarkable?

Looking up, he saw a couple of teenage girls aiming their phones at him and Lexie. He gave them a level stare. They flushed and turned around again.

Good. Lexie didn't need the stress of strangers gaping at her. She was under enough pressure with that.

Glancing at the time on his phone, he leaned toward her. The scent of her shampoo was becoming a familiar, comforting aroma.

"Lexie? We'll be arriving within an hour."

She looked up at him with a smile. "I'll be glad to get off this plane. Gavin, I wanted to thank you for helping me earlier. I really appreciated it. I don't know if I could have kept him steady by myself."

Gavin fought the irrational spurt of pride her words caused. He hadn't done anything spectacular. Although he was thankful that he was in the position to assist her. It felt good to know that she relied on him.

For a brief moment, he allowed himself the luxury of wondering what it would be like to be the man she relied on daily.

He shook his head. He was not a man that would make a good companion for a woman. He didn't have the charm of his brother. Plus, he was a cop.

Leo had always said it was a good thing he'd never married. Gavin tended to believe him, having lived with the man. A cop's life could be grueling. Not that he regretted becoming a cop. It was part of who he was.

It was no good wishing for a future with any woman. Not even one who seemed to get him the way Alexa did.

The moment they arrived at the hospital, Gavin could sense Alexa pulling away emotionally. The smile she'd worn that morning was gone, too, replaced by a blank look. Her gaze shifted neither right nor left. In fact, she walked with her chin up, her jaw set and her hands stuffed in her pockets. It was clear that they were also fisted.

The need to protect her rose up inside him. He only wished he knew what he needed to protect her from. The stares he met from the hospital employees were varied. Some were visibly curious, others were harried. No one looked at her with hostility. Wait. There was one person who looked at her angrily.

Uh-oh. The woman was coming closer.

"You have some nerve showing your face here." The woman pushed herself into Alexa's space, belligerent.

Lexie stiffened her already straight spine and stared the hostile woman down. "Chris. Always nice to see you, too."

"Ladies…"

Chris turned her angry face on him. "Stay out of it, hotshot."

"Not here, Chris. We have business with the shift supervisor."

The woman sneered. "Oh, sure. Or are you just too cowardly to face me after what you did?"

Eyes flashing, Lexie took a step forward, invading Chris's space. The other woman obviously didn't expect that. She stepped back, then colored furiously when she realized what she'd done. Lexie didn't back down, Gavin noticed, pride filling him. He would back her up, but this was clearly a fight she needed to take on herself. "I did nothing. I came home from a conference and found out that my fiancé was in the hospital."

"Because you drove him to it! I'm sure you were responsible for his death. Probably got careless with his meds."

"Nurse Stevens!" A strident voice whipped through the air. A tall, sturdy woman with salt-and-pepper hair tied up in a tight bun bore down on them. "You need to be about your shift. I hope I don't find that you are stirring up trouble. Again. You already have one reprimand on your record. These are my guests."

The woman's last name was Stevens? Like Brett Stevens? He narrowed his eyes and looked at her. He'd seen pictures of Brett. Chris resembled him a lot. Had to be his sister.

Lexie's eyes widened. "It was you who started the rumors that I'd killed Brett, wasn't it?" she asked Chris.

The woman started to open her mouth, no doubt to spit out more vitriol. He could see the storm gathering on her face. This was one rumor mill he could, and would, shut down.

"Nurse, one of the reasons we are here is that new evidence has surfaced. I'm assuming Brett was your brother?" She nodded, arms folded across her chest. Still belligerent, but she was listening. "We have new information that suggests your brother's suicide attempt was actually a botched attempted murder. Please don't hinder our investigation any longer. I'm sure you'd like to know the truth of what really happened."

Her face whitened. He didn't stay to give her a chance to say more. Gripping Lexie's elbow in a protective hold, he nodded at the administrator. She met his gaze then led the way to her office. Dr. Evelyn MacGuire was embossed on the nameplate sitting on the corner of her desk.

"I understand you have questions to ask, Sergeant Jackson," she said, gesturing for them to sit in the chairs in front of her desk.

"Yes, ma'am. It has come to our attention that Lexie—Nurse Grant—had a stalker here. We believe that he attempted to murder Brett Stevens, then attacked him a second time when he was in the hospital. After she left, the stalker followed her to LaMar Pond. He started working at the clinic where she works now under the assumed name of Dr. Henry Quinton, and is believed to be responsible for several attacks on her and some of her patients."

"I'm sorry, but the name Dr. Quinton is not

one that I'm familiar with, as I mentioned to your Chief Kennedy when he called here."

"Yes, ma'am. I'm aware of that. However, we have since learned that his name was not really Quinton. The man himself had disappeared. No doubt he's aware we know of his fake identity. What I was hoping is that I could show his picture to some of your staff. See if any of them can identify him."

"Let's not be too hasty. That might not be necessary."

"With all due respect, I'm sure the chief sent you his picture. Did you recognize him?"

She hesitated. Then her shoulders drooped slightly. "No, I did not recognize him. But then, I have only been here for a year. Miss Grant was already gone when I took this position."

Gavin stood up. He wanted her to know he meant business. "Dr. MacGuire, I have traveled from Pennsylvania on a matter that is literally life or death. I need to speak with members of your staff who were here at the time of Nurse Grant's employ. If I have to wait for a warrant to question your staff, someone else might die."

Fifteen minutes later, he was facing a number of the hospital staff. Nurses, doctors and the receptionist. Several of them kept throwing curious glances at Alexa. He gave them the rundown of what had been happening.

"Let's see that picture, Sergeant." One of the doctors held out his hand. He took the picture Gavin handed to him and peered at it closely. He shook his head. Several others did the same. The fourth person to look started to pass the picture on, then stopped.

"Wait a minute! This is Dr. Henry! I'm almost sure of it."

"Dr. Quinton's first name is Henry." Alexa's quiet voice broke in. At once, everyone wanted to see the photo again.

"I think you're right!" The first man squinted at the picture, holding his glasses closer to his eyes like a magnifying glass. "He shaved his head, added glasses. But it's Dr. Henry."

"When did you all last see him?" Now they were getting somewhere. Gavin could feel it.

"He didn't actually work here. He was a highly sought-after surgeon and speaker. Arrogant fellow, but brilliant. Great doctor. He visited a few times while giving seminars."

"Would he have had an opportunity to have met Nurse Grant?" Gavin asked.

"I'm sure he would have," one of the other

nurses said. "Or at least he would have seen her. Maybe. It's a definite possibility."

"Actually," another nurse spoke up, frowning, "he hasn't been here since Alexa left."

Gavin straightened. "Really?"

One of the doctors scratched his head. "That's right. He just sort of vanished."

"Why would a prominent doctor feel the need to assume a new identity?" Gavin asked the group.

"That's easy. The police were investigating him for the drowning death of his wife."

Gavin felt his eyes widen. "He was investigated? Did they ever find any evidence?"

The nurse who had offered the information shrugged her shoulders. "I have no idea. But it seems like he must have done it, right? Why run if he wasn't guilty?"

TWELVE

Gavin was absolutely convinced Dr. Quinton was Alexa's stalker.

"Here are the facts," he told Alexa when they were once again in Pennsylvania, heading back to his vehicle. "Dr. Quinton was under investigation as a suspect in the drowning death of his wife. I don't know if his fascination with you played into that. He did come looking for you and found a job where he could keep an eye on you."

Her phone pinged. Someone had messaged her through Facebook. It was Megan. She read it. And groaned.

"I can't believe this!"

That didn't sound good. "What?"

She shook her head. "I'm so embarrassed. Megan messaged me. Someone on the plane took a video of us helping the man who was choking and posted it on social media. It's going viral."

He remembered seeing people with their phones out on the plane.

He halted. She walked a few more steps before she saw that he wasn't following her.

"Gavin?"

"Hold on." He pulled out his phone and did a search on YouTube. What he found chilled him to the bone.

He didn't want to make her any more nervous than she already was, but she needed to be prepared. "Lexie, these pictures may have alerted Quinton that you went to Chicago with a cop. He's bound to figure out why. If he thinks you'll put two and two together, he's going to come after you even more viciously. Plus, look at this video."

He showed her the video posted on Facebook. "I saw this woman save a guy while heading to Chicago this morning on flight 2098."

Her mouth opened in a shocked O.

"It would not be too hard for Quinton to find out when flight 2098 landed in Chicago. And it wouldn't be too hard to find out what flights would be coming into Erie today," he told her.

"What do we do?"

He grabbed her hand and pulled her along. "It's a good thing I have my truck today. If he's watching for you, he'll be expecting you to be in a police car. We'd be caught unawares. As it is, we have been warned that he might know where we are. We know to be careful."

They almost made it to the station to pick up his cruiser. Almost. A mile away, they hit a red light. Traffic was practically nonexistent at this time of the evening. Gavin slowed the truck to a stop.

A burst of gunfire from the right hit the front end of the vehicle. Steam poured from under the hood with an explosive hiss. The needle on the coolant dial beginning rising.

"Lexie, down!"

She ducked, her knees banging the bottom of the glove compartment.

"Shots fired on Main Street!" he bellowed into his radio. "Officer and civilian under attack."

He kept down while he answered the dispatcher's questions, feeling like he was trapped in a cage. His truck wasn't going anywhere, and they couldn't see the gunman in the dark.

"Stay down, honey."

Lexie nodded at his warning. Her eyes caught his. There was fear there, but it was controlled. She was one of kind. Lacey would have freaked out. And he shouldn't compare Lexie with his former fiancée. The two women were nothing alike.

He glanced up. A cruiser would be there any minute.

It wasn't going to be enough. They might not have a minute just sitting there, and they couldn't drive without the radiator. Quinton wouldn't stop coming. They had to get out of the car.

A second shot hit the front tire. If the stalker hit Lexie's side of the truck just right, he'd get her. That was not a chance that Gavin was prepared to take.

"Come on! We can't stay here and be targets. We have to run!"

Pushing open the door, he leaped down, keeping the open door before him like a shield. Lexie slid across the seat and jumped down beside him. Her window shattered.

Grabbing her hand, he pulled her along the street, dodging in and out between the cars and buildings. She ran beside him. They had less than a mile to the police station. The sound of her panting as she struggled to keep up with him broke his heart. But he couldn't afford to let her rest.

Please, God. Let them make it.

A third shot erupted into the evening. Lexie cried out. He started to slow down.

"No, I'm okay." She was gasping in pain but kept running. "He grazed my hip. I'll be fine."

They continued running, their feet sloshing through the snow and slush. He felt bad, but there were several times when he was literally pulling Lexie along. He couldn't take the risk of stopping.

Ahead of him, a police car, sirens blaring, whipped around the corner. It raced past them. At the corner behind him, another cruiser joined in. Good.

A car pulled up beside them. "Get in," Lieutenant Willis ordered.

He pushed Lexie toward the cruiser, keeping himself between her and the shooter. Once inside the vehicle, they collapsed against the seat. That one had been much too close. The gunman was escalating again, shooting at them in the middle of town. If it had been earlier in the day, someone might have been seriously hurt.

"Lieutenant, drive by the hospital, will you? Lexie took a bullet to the hip."

Willis immediately changed course for the hospital. He expected Alexa to protest, but she seemed to be too exhausted. The lieutenant met his gaze in the rearview mirror.

"How's she holding up?"

Lexie stirred. "I'm good. Tired. And a little sore."

The sheer exhaustion in her voice tugged at Gavin. Reaching across the back seat, he looped his arm around her shoulders and gently pulled her to him. He nudged her head with his hand so that it was leaning against his shoulder. She sighed and closed her eyes.

"Rest on me for a bit. We'll be there soon."

She didn't respond. The urge to sweep the blond hair away from her face and kiss her forehead was strong. He resisted though. It wasn't appropriate, and besides, he didn't want Dan Willis to see him giving in to his emotions.

Not that Willis wouldn't understand. He remembered very well how the lieutenant's own wife had been in danger several years earlier.

Why had he just compared his relationship with Lexie to Willis's with his wife? There was no way that he had a future with the beautiful woman snuggled up against his side. He might want one. But he had learned long ago that wanting something did not mean you'd get it.

Lexie's hip needed five stitches. He held her hand all the way back to the station. Honestly though, he wasn't sure if it was to comfort him or her. Seeing her injured had twisted him up inside in a way he couldn't remember feeling since Leo died.

They'd just sat down in the chief's office when her cell phone rang.

Glancing at the number, she frowned.

"Who is it?" he asked her.

"I have no idea. I've never seen this number before."

She answered the call, putting it on speaker.

"Hello? This is Alexa Grant."

"Alexa?" a soft feminine voice gasped out. Alexa's frown deepened. She didn't look concerned. More like puzzled. "I need help," the woman said.

"I'm sorry. I don't know who this is."

"It's Linda. Linda King."

Lexie inhaled sharply.

"Linda! Where are you? Are you hurt?" Her voice had taken on a sharp edge.

"*Nee*. I am not hurt. I am calling from the community phone. I am scared. I saw him. I saw the man who shot Marvin. I was behind the barn and I saw him. I thought he saw me, and I ran. I am scared he will come for me."

* * *

A grim moment of silence filled the room when Lexie disconnected the phone. Her heart ached for Linda. To see her brother shot and to be chased by the man who did it.

"Miss Grant," the chief addressed her. The tone in his voice made her think she wasn't going to like what he had to say. "I think it would be best if I had one of the officers take you back to the safe house. They can stay with you until—"

"Chief Kennedy." Lexie interrupted the man. Gavin stared at her. She grimaced. People probably didn't argue with the chief of police as a rule. "I am sorry to argue, sir, but I really think it would be better if I came along."

The chief raised his brow. "I don't see how dragging a civilian along would be helpful."

"Lexie," Gavin began.

She shut him down with a glare. He backed away, hands up. She switched her attention back to the chief. She had to make this man understand.

"Sir, I know Linda King. I know what she looks like. Do you? Plus, she knows me and trusts me. I was the one she called, not the police. And she won't call the police. It's not the Amish way. I don't know if she would even agree to talk with you. But if we find her, she might talk with me."

"She has a point, Chief," Gavin commented.

The chief ran his hand along his chin, thinking. Finally, he nodded. "I can see that what you say makes sense. I don't like it. But right now, my concern is locating that young woman and keeping her safe."

A few minutes later, Lexie was once again riding next to him in his cruiser. His presence was an anchor for her.

Linda King was no longer at the community phone booth when they arrived. The small phone booth that held the only phone the Amish community had for emergencies was empty. It was literally a small wooden shed, large enough for one person, with a phone like one would find in an old-fashioned phone booth.

They'd come in force this time. The police were taking no chances that a single officer would be taken down by a sniper.

"These footprints look fresh, sir," Gavin said, squatting outside the booth and examining the prints that were in the new snow. Alexa stayed back, not wanting to add more footprints than necessary and hamper the investigation.

Chief Kennedy came closer to Gavin.

"They head out in that direction, toward the woods."

As a group, the officers and Alexa headed for the trees. The snow was thinner in the wooded area, and it was harder to make out any tracks. There was no sign of Linda.

"Spread out," the chief directed. "The girl may be around here, and she may be injured. We're also keeping an eye out for our sniper, the man most of you know of as Dr. Quinton. Use your radios for important communications. Otherwise, let's keep radio silence."

The search parties spread out. Alexa found herself between Dan Willis and Gavin. It was harder to see because it was dark outside. Their twin flashlights cut through the blackness, shooting beams of light through the trees.

The temperature was dropping. They searched for over an hour. Alexa's teeth were chattering. The warmth of her gloves and boots had long since faded. Both were now wet and soggy. Every minute, it was harder and harder to lift her feet and trudge through the mud, slush and snow.

The radios crackled to life. Sergeant Ryan Parker's voice sliced through the stillness. "I am on the next road to the north of the house. I have found an empty buggy."

Alexa stopped in her tracks. Linda might have come in a buggy. It would have made sense. She didn't live close enough to the phone booth to walk, not at this time of night.

Dan decided to pull their team over to the buggy. In the few minutes it took to get there, Alexa tried to keep her mind from thinking about what might have happened to Linda. She didn't know the girl that well. She was very shy. She was only about seventeen years old.

Linda had been courting last year. Her fiancé had been killed in a farm accident last summer. She and Marvin were all that was left of their family. Now he was in the hospital fighting for his life and she was...what? Hiding? A prisoner? She thought about all the people the stalker had hurt. Noah. Marvin. Eli. He'd even struck Waneta, Eli's wife. She wouldn't be surprised if he went after someone who could identify him.

Someone like sweet Linda King.

When they arrived at the buggy, all the hope she'd held that they would find the girl, or that the buggy would belong to someone else, vanished like smoke.

"That horse." She pointed to the mare with

a distinctive star on its face. "That horse is owned by the Kings. This is Linda's buggy."

The officers digested the information in grim silence. One of them, Lieutenant Tucker, she thought, got out his phone and started taking pictures of the horse and the inside of the buggy.

Chief Kennedy looked more severe than she'd ever seen him. "Are you positive that this is the right horse?"

"One hundred percent." She pointed at the star on the mare's face. "That mark is so unique. I have seen it several times."

The tense silence stretched as the officers searched the area for any sign of struggle or clues.

"Chief!"

Gavin was squatting, flashing his light under the buggy.

"What do you have, Jackson?"

Instead of answering, Gavin shifted his weight. He moved so that the chief would have a better view, she realized. Leaning to the side, she peered under the buggy, straining to see what he was pointing to. When she saw it, her blood ran cold.

On the ground, lying in a patch of mud, was the stalker's signature red rose.

Dr. Quinton had Linda.

THIRTEEN

It took the team the better part of the night to search the area. Alexa waited in Gavin's police car for most of it. One of the officers was constantly nearby, standing guard.

Sighing, she planted her elbows on her knees and leaned forward so her face was cupped in her hands. She was so tired. And so worried. Who'd be next? Her eyes flashed to where Gavin was even now pacing outside the vehicle, talking on the radio. If something happened to him, it would devastate her.

Her feelings were so powerful, so deep, that she could hardly breathe at the thought of going back to a life without him. However, he was a cop, so he'd always be in danger. Did she want to deal with that stress in her life?

Yes. It was either that, or not having him in her life at all. Even if she could only be with him a short time, she'd take it. The only problem was, he'd made it clear that he intended to keep to his solitary ways.

Maybe when all this was over, and life returned back to normal, maybe she'd tell him how she felt.

Right. And watch him run in the opposite direction. The man was honorable and steady to the core. He also had a chip on his shoulder and a habit of taking responsibility for things that were not his fault. Things like his uncle's death.

But wasn't she guilty of holding on to things, too?

She remembered her anger at her mother. At her father. Even at her brother. Who was that anger hurting besides herself? Her mother couldn't feel it, her father didn't care, and Allen...

She frowned. She didn't actually know how Allen felt. Because she'd shut him out. She'd always thought that when he asked her to come to live with him he didn't really mean it. But had she given him a chance? Now she wondered how he would react if she told him what was happening. He might not even care. But he might. *And you're not giving him the chance to show you.*

Slowly she pulled her phone out of her

pocket and tapped in his number. He probably wouldn't answer. He had to be busy. She could call back.

"Hello? Alex?" he answered.

He'd always called her Alex. She hated it, but now a smile bloomed on her face at the pet name. "Hey, big brother."

"Sis! It's great to hear your voice! Melissa told me just this morning that I needed to insist you come for Christmas this year. No excuses."

She couldn't speak for a moment around the lump in her throat. He did care. And he wanted her to visit.

"Alex?"

"That would be great, Allen. Tell her I'd love to come. I can't wait to see my little niece, too." She paused. Then she took a deep breath. She needed to tell him. "Listen, Allen. There's something I have to tell you."

He must have heard the serious tone in her voice. "You can tell me anything you want. Always."

Ten minutes later, there were tears running down her face. Her brother was outraged on her behalf. He was all set to get on an airplane the next day and come to her rescue. She'd never given him the chance to play her hero before. She'd always assumed that he wouldn't want to. She also realized that she might have misjudged her sister-in-law. She could hear Melissa in the background telling Allen to ask her to come stay with them until the danger was gone.

"You don't need to come yet, Allen. The police are on it. I even have my own personal cop keeping an eye on me." She blushed just talking about it. Good thing he couldn't see her face now.

"Tell me about your cop." Her brother's voice had calmed down. Now she heard the brotherly tease in it.

Her cop. Not quite. But she liked the way it sounded.

"He's not my cop. His name is Gavin. He keeps an eye on me, that's all."

"Sis. You can protest all you want. But I can hear the way your voice changes when you talk about him."

What was she supposed to say to that?

"Anyway," she said, changing the subject, "you don't need to come now. I appreciate your willingness to do so. I really do."

"I will come anytime you need me, sis. Anytime. All you need to do is call."

For the first time, she believed him.

After she disconnected the call, she sat for

a moment, feeling warm. He did care. After all these years of doubting, she finally knew the truth.

Something hard thumped against the car.

She looked up, startled. Gavin had fallen against the car. What was wrong with him? A second later, she knew. A shot hit the edge of the car. Was he hurt? Scrambling out the other side, she crawled around to him. He was crouched down, his gun out. He was speaking urgently into the radio. He saw her and a fierce frown covered his face.

"Get in the car."

She didn't answer. Now that she was beside him, she could tell that he was not injured.

The officers who had heard the shots swarmed the area. They were searching for the sniper in the dark. A car careened down the street. It had to have been pushing eighty.

"Get in!" Gavin ground out again, then he got behind the wheel. She was still buckling her seat belt when the engine roared to life and he hit the sirens. He took off after the fleeing sniper; he started to swerve onto the main road.

"Wait!" she shouted.

"What?" he said, looking around.

"There! Over near the bridge. I thought I saw someone."

She didn't dare give voice to the hope that was in her mind.

He narrowed his eyes. "I don't see anything."

Still, he turned the wheel and headed toward the bridge. They had to get out and walk. As they got closer, she could hear a ragged sound. Intuitively she reached forward and took Gavin's hand. She didn't even try to tell herself it was because it was hard to see in the dark. It would be a lie. She took his hand because he made her feel safe. To her surprise, he didn't shake her off. Instead, she felt his warm fingers tighten around hers.

The sound became more pronounced as they drew closer It was someone breathing. She knew what they'd find before they rounded the corner. Linda King was huddled on the ground next to the bridge. Gavin flashed the light over her, careful not to shine the beam directly into her face. No obvious injuries were visible.

"Linda? It's Alexa Grant."

With a sob, the Amish teenager threw herself forward into Alexa's arms. Alexa stumbled back. Gavin was at her shoulder in a second to steady her. She was shocked by the girl's actions. It was totally out of character. She must have been beyond terrified to act this way.

"Linda, we thought that he'd caught you. The man who shot your brother."

Linda stopped crying and moved back. "He did. I saw him and ran to my buggy. I knew I had to go fast. He was faster, and he hit me." She touched her cheek with her hand. "I had a shovel in the buggy. I was bringing it to my friend. It was on the ground. He stepped on it, and it came up and smacked him here," Linda said, pointing to an eye. "He yelled, and I ran. I have been hiding for a long time."

They drove her to her neighbor's house to stay. The other officers were chasing after Quinton.

At her friends' house, Linda stood in the doorway, watching them with shadowed eyes. She was uncertain if she would come to the police station to give a description. All she knew was that he was medium height and had some kind of dark glasses on. He wore a hood, so she couldn't tell if he was bald or not.

"Alexa, be careful. This man, he is not a *gut* man. He wants you dead. I heard what he said to my brother before he shot him. He told him that you were his." She turned her eyes to Gavin. "He will kill you because you are with her. That's why he shot my brother. He shot him because he saw Alexa and Marvin standing together. I heard him say that he was watching her. All the time."

She understood what the woman was saying. Any man who talked with her, stood near her, was a target. She already knew that.

"Maybe I should leave," Alexa whispered to Gavin. "Maybe if I left, he would stop targeting the people here."

Gavin frowned at her. "How would that help? Lexie, the man has already changed his identity and his appearance once. What would stop him from doing it again? And his behavior has escalated to the point where no one is really safe from him. People with obsessions like his don't lose their focus. He'll just keep coming after you. We have to stop him now."

Gavin didn't like the look on Lexie's face. The glance she threw his way was an odd mixture of fear and agony. He knew what she was thinking. She was thinking that she was putting others in danger. As usual, others were foremost in her thoughts.

That was one of the reasons he admired her.

She was one of a kind.

And he had to let her go.

He'd never faced anything more painful in his life.

His radio beeped. The dispatcher's voice split the silence. "Structure fire at the LaMar Pond Warehouse on Main Street. Smoke has been spotted at the scene. Unknown entrapment. Arson is suspected."

"That's right next to the clinic!" Alexa said, grabbing hold of his arm.

It was the stalker. Quinton set fire to another building. He knew it. Who else would it be?

"Come on, Lexie. It's time to go. It's got to be our guy."

She jogged to the cruiser next to him. He placed a hand on her back briefly before she moved around to her side of the vehicle. He couldn't explain it, the need to touch her, just to reassure himself of her continued well-being. They made it to the scene of the blaze in good time. The fire department was already on the scene. Thick black smoke poured from a broken window in the back of the building. So far, it looked like the clinic had not been damaged.

Getting out, they joined the fire chief. He was listening to the information coming in. "The fire is contained in the back storage room. There's no doubt that it was arson,

Chief. There was a pile of flammable material, just stacked, and some kind of accelerant was dumped on top. My gut instinct says gas, but we'll know for sure soon."

The chief started to respond. Suddenly there was another voice yelling in the background. "We have a body here! Someone was trapped in the fire."

Gavin winced. That was one of the things that emergency responders feared. Arriving on a scene and finding that they were too late to save a civilian. He felt Lexie move up behind him. Part of him wanted to shield her from this mess. That would be ridiculous. She was a nurse. She had probably seen much worse. Still, he wanted to keep her safe. Where could he have her go? He needed to get more information.

"Lexie, I need to see what I can do to help. And I need to document the scene."

She glanced around, a slight frown creating ridges on her forehead. When she looked back at him, her eyes were determined. "Can I help?"

"I don't know. Stay with me."

The paramedics and the firefighters dealt with the body that had been found in the storage room. It looked like he had been trapped and something had hit him on the head.

Gavin talked with Chief Kennedy. "It looks to me like our perp got to the guy before the fire started. Hit him with something. The fire hadn't spread very far when it was contained. So I have trouble believing that whatever hit him burned up in the blaze."

His chief nodded, his hand rubbing the scruff on his chin.

Gavin continued. "This is how I see it. The perp kills him, whoever he was, then sets the fire to cover up the crime."

"I hear a 'but' coming, Sergeant."

Gavin spun and paced a few feet away and back, rubbing his hands together as he thought. "It doesn't fit. You know? He's made no effort to cover up his other attacks. He did them right out in the open. So why cover up this one?"

A man ran toward them. "Chief Kennedy. Sergeant Jackson. I think we might have something."

He held out a piece of darkened, twisted metal.

"What exactly is that?" the chief asked.

"It was part of a homemade explosive. It appears that he was in the middle of setting the blaze, and this went off prematurely."

Gavin blinked. "He blew himself up?"

"Yep."

Wow. He would not have expected that in a million years. The killer had been a step ahead of them the whole time. To get killed in his own trap seemed anticlimactic, somehow.

"Do we have any proof that this is Quinton? Or that he was involved in the arson case in Chicago?"

The chief raised his brows. "You tell me. You're the one who went there."

"Nothing seemed to connect him to that crime. We can place him at the hospital one time during Lexie's time of employment there. We have nothing to place him at the flower shop, so it might be a coincidence..."

His voice dropped off.

"Except that you don't believe in coincidences."

"It would be a really weird coincidence," Lexie's voice interrupted. "Especially since the man stalking me sent me flowers from there. Not just once, but several times."

He'd forgotten she was listening. But she was right. "It would be a weird coincidence. Which in my mind, means there's a link somewhere. We just haven't found it yet."

"But you will." She gazed up at him, utter

faith in her eyes. He felt humbled. Catching the chief's amused glance, he flushed.

A firefighter ran out of the building.

"Everyone get back!" One of the firefighters ran out from the back of the building. "There's another bomb. It's gonna blow!"

Gavin didn't hesitate. He grabbed hold of Lexie and pushed her back behind his car, then he covered her body with his. And not a second too soon. A second explosion rocked the building. He could feel his cruiser rock as the force from the blast hit it. Chunks of burning wood flew everywhere. One landed inches from them.

The firefighters and the police officers who had responded were kept busy for the next few hours. The warehouse was a total loss. Parts of the building were burning and smoldering, other parts looking as if they had melted. It was a good thing that the fire had happened when no one was on duty. He wondered about the man inside the building. Had it truly been the arsonist? Or was it another victim? He'd have to wait to find out what the investigators found. It would have been tragic had any innocent lives been lost in the blaze.

The immediate worry was the clinic. It was separated from the warehouse by less than thirty feet. They needed to keep the blaze from spreading. Quite a feat, Gavin thought, watching the sparks and chunks of burning debris getting caught in the breeze and blowing toward the clinic. He helped, keeping a water hose on the clinic, dousing it with water to keep the fire from catching.

By the time the fire was completely out and the other buildings declared safe, the sun was rising. Gavin went to his cruiser and found Lexie curled up on the seat, sound asleep. She'd been a trouper, working alongside them, doing whatever needed done.

Reaching over, he gently pulled the seat belt out and buckled her in. He tried to do it without waking her. She stirred anyway. Those blue-gray eyes fluttered open and stared at him.

He was so thankful that she was safe. She was dirty, her hair and clothes smelled like smoke, making his cruiser thick with the odor, too. He didn't care. She had survived.

He started to move closer to her. Stopped himself. *Don't get too close, Jackson. She's not for you.* He did, however, allow himself the luxury of running a finger down her smudged cheek. The right corner of her lips turned up. She sighed. Sleepy, she was unguarded. His breath stuck in his throat at the emotion in her gaze. It was as if someone had punched him in the stomach. The last thing he'd wanted to do was to cause her pain.

He had to close this case. Their lives, and their hearts, depended on it.

FOURTEEN

The next day was one of the longest Gavin could ever remember. He went to work, doing his best to stay on top of things. In his mind, he kept seeing Lexie as she'd looked last night in his cruiser.

He knew that he had never felt so strongly for anyone. And he had no hope.

He would not go to see her after work, he decided. She was protected. As soon as the body from the fire was identified, they'd know if Quinton was really dead and the threat gone. Then she could go home. He wouldn't need to be by her side all the time.

Instead of being relieved, he was hollow.

He was clearing off his desk, getting ready to head out, when his phone rang. It was Chuck Burch, the medical examiner. Despair and hope warred inside his chest.

Gavin deliberately forced himself to push

his emotions down, deep where they couldn't interfere with his duty. Then he walked to the chief's office.

"Jackson," the chief greeted him, sitting back in his chair. "What can I do for you?"

"I just wanted to let you know that the coroner's office called. The man from the fire was Quinton."

Paul Kennedy stood and came around his desk. "Are you going to go to let Miss Grant know?"

Staring into his chief's eyes, Gavin knew that he hadn't been able to hide his emotions from his boss. Sympathy shone brightly in his gaze. And a question.

"Um, actually, sir, I thought you would call to let her know."

"Gavin, that's not what I would have expected from you. She deserves to hear the news from you."

He thought the chief might mean more than just Quinton's death. His chief was challenging him about his intentions toward her. Shifting his feet, he could not think of a suitable reply.

"I know what you can do," the chief said.

"What?"

Chief Kennedy clapped him on the shoulder. "I have two cats at my house that don't belong to me," he drawled. "I would be very much obliged if you would get them and take Miss Grant her cat. I'm sure the animal will be a very welcome surprise."

He really couldn't say no. As he strode out of the station, there was a sense of eagerness in his steps. He had planned to go home without seeing her. But now, realizing that he had the chance to see her, even if it was for the last time, had anticipation zipping through his soul.

When he arrived at the Kennedy house, he found that Irene had the cats already in their crates. "Paul told me you were coming," she greeted him.

"Hey, Irene. I hear congrats are in order."

She smiled so wide, he couldn't help but grin back. "Yes, but the boys don't know yet. We're going to tell them soon. So don't spill the beans, okay?"

"Yes, ma'am!" Jackson gave Irene a mock salute. She laughed and made to move one of the crates. "Hey, none of that! I've got it."

She rolled her eyes but didn't protest. Soon he had two cats stowed in the back of his cruiser. They tried to outdo each other with pitiful yowling meows. He grinned to himself. It would be an interesting drive.

He got a call from Zee. "Hey, Jackson. I just

dropped Alexa off at her house. Chief said that the coroner had IDed our perp."

"Good to know." He hung up and gave the crates in the back a quick glance in the mirror. "Okay, Cinnamon. You're on your way home."

He grew uneasy as he approached Alexa's house. What would he say to her? *Hey, it's been a blast but I don't do relationships?*

He snorted in disgust.

All too soon, he was sitting in her driveway. Taking a deep breath, he opened his door and got out of the car. Grabbing Cinnamon's crate, he sauntered to the front door, working to keep his expression neutral.

He'd barely knocked when she swung open the door, pleasure illuminating her face when she saw him. Then she slid her gaze to the crate in his hand. The happy shriek she let out destroyed his neutral expression. The grin was on his face before he could stop it.

She grabbed the crate and pulled it inside. Then she reached back and pulled him in by his hand and shut the door behind him. He could have resisted. He should have. But he didn't.

He wanted to be by her side so much, and he knew that he couldn't.

"I should—"

"Gavin, thank you so much for bringing my baby home."

He blinked. Her baby. He glanced at the fat purring feline in her arms. "Big baby."

Then there was sudden silence. Awkward silence. They both knew he'd come to say goodbye, he realized. He could read the sorrow that suddenly darkened her face. And the hope that she held on to. The cat leaped down from his perch in her arms.

It was no use. He couldn't do it, couldn't let her hope when there was none.

She shifted. Moved to the side. He knew what would happen before it did. She lifted her right foot. And accidentally stepped on Cinnamon's tail. The large cat yowled, and Lexie jumped. She nearly fell over. He made the mistake of catching hold of her, to steady her.

For just a moment, he stopped resisting. The moment he leaned forward, she rose up on her toes. Their lips met. Held.

He moved back. Her face glowed up at him. Unable to think why he wasn't stopping, he kissed her again. It was a kiss that sparkled and glittered in his mind. In his soul. A kiss that he'd remember all his life.

It was all he could ever have.

He stepped back. He was letting her go.

* * *

Alexa opened her eyes, still dazzled by the kiss that had rocked her senses.

The dazzled feeling lasted only until she caught the light of self-reproach on Gavin's face. He was regretting kissing her. She knew he was, and it hurt. More than that, it made her angry.

"That shouldn't have happened," Gavin muttered, confirming her suspicions. He stepped back from her. Her arms dropped from his shoulders and flapped to her sides. She wrapped them around herself. His sudden distance made her feel cold from the inside out.

"Why shouldn't it have happened, Gavin?" she challenged him, lifting her chin. "You can't tell me that you don't have feelings for me. I know you do."

He moved farther away, then he turned his back to her. His posture emanated frustration. He was completely shutting her out.

"I'm not good for you, Lexie. I'm a cop. I live a dangerous life. A life that I chose, but I have no right forcing it on any woman."

"Isn't it my choice if I can accept your job? Besides, I'm not asking you to marry me. Just for the chance for us to get to know each other better."

She knew immediately that she'd said the wrong thing.

"I can't do it, Lexie. Not again. The last time I let a woman get too close, she stayed until she found a better man. I won't open myself up to that again."

"Don't you dare compare me to your sister-in-law. I would never play with a man's feelings that way."

He pivoted back to her, and his face softened slightly as his eyes scanned her face. Almost like he was memorizing what she looked at. He was really going to do it. He was actually going to walk away from her.

"Of course, I know that you wouldn't play with my feelings, Lexie. But I still don't know if I can take the chance again. You can do better than me. I'm a good cop. And I have accepted that that will be my life."

Suddenly she gave up trying to reason with him. He had made her too mad. "Do you even believe the faith you profess?" she questioned.

His jaw dropped. "What are you talking about?"

She glared. "You say you believe, but isn't this really still about your brother and your parents, and the fact that you can't forgive them? That you won't forgive them?"

He stiffened, but she ignored him. She wasn't finished. Not by a long shot.

"You gave me that Bible, and I have been reading it. But now I wonder if you really read it. You know that your uncle had made notes in the Bible. Did you ever read them? I read them." She ran to the table and picked up the book and flipped through to the Gospel of Matthew. She knew it was in here somewhere. She found his uncle's now familiar scrawl. "Here. The Sermon on the Mount. The Lord's Prayer. Right next to where it says, '"And forgive us our debts, as we forgive our debtors."' Your uncle wrote, '"Lord, please soften G.'s heart to forgive his brother."'

She shut the book and aimed a level stare at the man who aggravated her like no other. The man who held her heart in his hands and was so set on breaking it.

"He was praying for you to forgive your brother, Gavin. Not for him. But for you. I have read other notes. Your inability to forgive is hurting him, but it's hurting you more. Let it go."

She saw the vulnerable look on his face, and for a moment she thought she'd gotten through to him. Then his expression hardened, his eyes became shuttered. The invisible wall he had built between them was practically tangible. She'd given her best and failed.

He shook her head. "I'm sorry, Lexie. I really am. But this is who I am. And my brother is who he is. He betrayed me once. How could I ever know that he wouldn't do so again?"

"Gavin, please. People can change, can't they? Give him a chance."

He didn't answer. He gave her one last sad glance then walked out the door. She listened as he started his car and drove away. He was gone. She slumped against the door, too broken to cry. Cinnamon wound around her legs, meowing mournfully. Even the cat knew something was wrong.

The next day she waited, hoping he'd call. Admit he was wrong. But he didn't.

He was truly gone.

The phone rang around six. She jumped up and ran to where she'd left it sitting on the counter. Maybe it was Gavin. She eagerly looked at the number. It was the LaMar Pond PD.

She swiped a trembling finger across the screen to unlock it. "Hello?" She held her breath. *Please be Gavin. Please be Gavin.*

"Alexa, Ryan Parker here."

She let her breath out, closing her eyes in disappointment.

"Alexa? You there?"

"Yes, hi. What's up?" She straightened her shoulders. She was not some weak woman who couldn't survive without a man. *Get control of yourself, Alexa.*

"Hey, Jackson asked me to call you. The clinic's all clear to reopen. You can go back to your normal activities."

Was it her imagination, or could she hear the question in his voice? Why wasn't Gavin calling her himself?

She shook her head. Forced a bright note into her voice she so wasn't anywhere near feeling. "That's great to know. Thanks so much for telling me!"

"Sure, anytime." There was a pause. "I shouldn't say this, but I saw him today, and he looks miserable."

Tears that she promised herself she wouldn't cry filled her eyes. "I can't do anything about that, Ryan. He's got to work through this. I did my best."

"Don't give up on him. He'll come around."

She gave a noncommittal response and hung up the phone.

She had her life back. She could go to work,

come home without fear and carry on as she had before her life collided with Gavin Jackson. She should be celebrating. Instead, she sat on the couch, holding her cat to her chest and burying her face in his fur, letting her agony and grief flow out of her in a tide of tears.

It was awfully hard to celebrate when there was a hole in her chest in the shape of Gavin.

FIFTEEN

Would Gavin call today?

Of course not. He'd been very clear that they could never be together. She couldn't decide which emotion was stronger—anger at him for being so stubborn, or sadness that he was so determined to be alone.

"Did you hear that Marvin King's going to live?" Megan asked, setting a stack of files next to her computer.

"I did hear that." She had nearly cried tears of joy when she heard he was going to survive. They hadn't heard anything on Eli Schwartz yet. Noah, however, was home and recovering nicely. She'd received a package from Naomi filled with a variety of home-baked cookies in thanksgiving. Alexa didn't have the heart to tell the woman that she couldn't eat them.

She'd brought them in to the clinic to share.

Between Sam, the janitor—Damien—and Megan, they'd been gone in under two days.

The door to the clinic opened. Alexa looked up. A smile broke across her face.

"Linda! We were just talking about your brother. I'm so glad he's going to be all right!"

The smile melted off her face as the Amish girl hurried over. She wasn't just in a hurry. She was upset. Something was wrong.

"Linda! What's wrong? Is it Marvin?" Fear churned. What if he'd had a relapse?

"He is *gut*." Reaching the desk, Linda slapped a newspaper onto the desk. It was several days old. "This is the problem."

Alexa and Megan both flicked their eyes to where Linda was pointing. It was an article about Dr. Quinton, who hadn't really been Dr. Quinton, but was a fugitive, after running to avoid the police, who were investigating him for the drowning death of his wife. The details of the stalking and his past crimes were all enumerated.

"What do you mean this is wrong, Linda? What's wrong about it?"

Linda brushed her fingers over the picture of Dr. Quinton. "This is not the man I saw that day at my house. This was not the man who shot my brother."

Silence met her words. If the now deceased doctor hadn't been the shooter, then who had been? Her eyes skimmed the waiting room. It was full today, being the first day open since the bombing a week ago. Plus, it was right before Christmas. The patients knew they'd have to wait until after the holiday to get seen if they waited. Word had obviously gotten around. They'd come in droves that morning.

Now their lives might be at risk.

A chill struck her heart. It had to be someone in the clinic. Someone who knew her schedule and her patients. There weren't many men, here, though.

She grabbed her cell phone out of her pocket. "I'll call Gavin. He's a cop. He'll know what to do."

Her fingers began to tap in the number. Strong fingers plucked the phone from her hands. Startled, she looked up into the cold dark eyes of the janitor, Damien Alexander. She'd never noticed how hard his eyes were.

It was him. He was the man who was stalking her. The man who had killed for her. She couldn't remember ever seeing him before he started working at the clinic.

Stay calm. Maybe you're wrong. She knew she wasn't though.

"Damien." She gave an uncomfortable laugh. "What are you doing? I need a phone to call my friend."

Damien shoved something into her side. She didn't have to look to know it was a gun. Megan gasped.

"You!" Linda said. "You were the one!"

He sent an almost bored glance her way. "Yes, yes, I'm the one who shot your brother. It's an unfortunate fact of growing up in the city that I'm not a very good shot. But I think I can manage at this close range. Now, if you would be so kind, I would hate to shoot your friend this way. Come around into the hallway. And don't say anything."

Linda obeyed. Gesturing with his gun, he pushed the three women back into the farthest examination room. Dr. Jackson was there, finishing his dictation from his last patient.

"What's the meaning of this—" he began but ceased speaking when he saw the gun. Damien ignored him.

The first thing the janitor did was to confiscate the rest of the cell phones.

"I can't have youse guys calling anyone, can I?" That's when Alexa heard his Chicago accent for the first time.

He turned to Megan. "Your keys."

Megan handed him the keys she had to the rooms. Ironically, Damien had the other set of keys. He moved to the door. "I'm going to get rid of our guests. If I hear any noise, one of them will die."

Seeing the chilling expression on his face, Alexa believed he would do exactly what he claimed. The others must have agreed, for once the door was shut and locked behind him, no one said a single word.

Alexa had no hope that Gavin would discover the truth of the situation. As far as he and everyone else had been concerned, Dr. Quinton had been their stalker. She didn't blame anyone for the wrong conclusion. She'd believed it herself.

The lock rattled. Damien slipped back inside, an almost pleasant look on his face. "Now, isn't this cozy?" His eyes settled on Alexa. "I must say, I never planned to have such a large crowd for our final meeting."

At the words *final meeting*, Alexa felt the blood rush from her head. Beside her, Megan sobbed out a soft breath. Linda was silent. Oddly, Sam was quiet, too. She'd gotten used to his rather boastful personality. It surprised her that he wouldn't have something to say at a time like this.

Gavin would have, she thought. Not to hear himself talk. No, Gavin would have drawn all the attention to himself to keep Damien's focus, and the gun, off everyone else. Well, she could do the same thing. He was after her, so maybe she'd be able to hold his attention until someone noticed something amiss and came to help.

Which wasn't likely; she knew that, but she had to try.

"Damien, why? I don't understand."

As she'd planned, his focus jerked to stare at her. He sneered. It was an ugly expression on what should have been a handsome face. She barely managed to hold back the shudder.

"You don't understand. That's rich. This has all been for you. I came into the hospital after I'd had a chemical burn. You treated me, and I knew you were the one. But you couldn't be faithful, could you?" He spat on the ground. She flinched. "You had to go and get engaged to that pitiful fellow. I poisoned him. It was so easy. But that didn't work. He was found and rushed to the hospital. Then you showed up. You still didn't understand that you were mine. I took care of him."

The shudder that she'd been suppressing worked its way through her. She kept her face blank with effort. He was talking in front of witnesses. If they survived this, there would be three people beside herself to testify against him.

"I didn't know you. Surely you knew that?"

"You never gave me a second glance," he shouted. "Then you moved. Away from me. I followed you. It was ridiculously easy to get a job here. The doctor never even checked my references."

Probably because he himself was illegally practicing.

"I thought you'd see me in this joke of a town. Then I saw you flirting with all the men who came in. I had to step in. Don't you see that? I had to save you from yourself. Then you started hanging out with that cop."

His voice grew angry.

"I saw you! Riding in his car. Letting him take the rose I gave you. As if it was nothin'." He was getting so worked up now, spittle flew from his mouth as he continued to rant. "And then you let him kiss you!"

Her stomach lurched. He had been watching! The perfect moment she'd enjoyed with Gavin, thinking she was safe in the privacy of her home, had been an illusion. Damien had been peeping on them! Out of the corner of her eye, she saw Sam shift. She ignored him.

When Damien waved the gun toward her, she pulled back. The reaction seemed to enrage him further. "See how stupid you are! Even now, you are here thinking that you are too good for me. I saw you pull back. You won't be so high and mighty when you watch your friends here die. One by one."

Please, God, no! Please protect them.

"Damien, they have nothing to do with this. Let them go. Please. They're innocent."

He laughed at that. "Innocent? Doll, no one's innocent. That one, there—" he pointed at Megan "—she's been flirting with me."

Megan paled. She hadn't been doing more than being kind, Alexa knew. Megan was friendly, and bubbly, but she didn't flirt.

"And that dude over there, he thinks he's so important 'cause he's the doctor. Yeah, well, so was the quack who was here before him. I killed Quinton, and I can kill him, too. I'll enjoy it."

"Why would you hurt Dr. Quinton?"

"Because he had found my pictures. The ones I had taken of you."

She remembered the pictures.

"I knew he was gonna fire me. When I shot

that first guy, Quinton suspected me. Oh, he never came out and said it, but I knew he did. I couldn't chance that he would turn me in to the police. So I took care of him. Then I planted the pictures in his locker, knowing that the cops would focus on finding him." He looked thoughtful for a moment. "I really miss my pictures."

He shrugged.

"My next girlfriend's gonna appreciate me, I can promise you that."

He raised the gun again.

What was Lexie doing right now? Was she at work? Was she thinking about him?

Gavin slammed down his coffee cup so hard, some of the steaming liquid slopped over the side and onto his desk, spattering the papers he had spread there. Growling, he grabbed a tissue from the box on the file cabinet and mopped the mess up.

He felt eyes watching him. Glancing up, he encountered the startled gazes of both Zee and Parker. Zee quickly averted her eyes. Not Parker. He sauntered over to Gavin's desk and hiked a hip to sit on the edge. Then he waited.

Gavin thought about ignoring his pal but decided against it. No one had more patience than Ryan Parker. He'd sit and wait it out until Gavin gave in.

"Is there something you wanna say, Parker?" Leaning back in his chair, Gavin tried to pull off casual and unconcerned. He could tell that Parker wasn't buying it, though.

"Out with it, Jackson. I can see something's eating at you. And has been since yesterday. What's up? Although I can probably guess."

What was that supposed to mean?

He opened his mouth to deny that anything was wrong. But the strength of his frustration got the better of him. He needed to get it out there, off his chest. It was burning a hole in him.

"It's Lexie. I know that all the evidence points to the doctor. And I know that it looks like his death was an accident. I just can't see it happening that way. It's too perfect."

Parker considered his words. When he nodded, Gavin's heart sank. He had really wanted to believe that he was being paranoid.

"I will agree it seems too neat. But if Dr. Quinton wasn't the stalker, who was?"

Making a snap decision, Gavin bounded to his feet. "Hold on."

A minute later, he was in the chief's office, explaining his theory.

"Jackson," the chief said, the drawl missing. "If you're right, and I am not in any way discounting your theory, but if you're right, then Miss Grant is still in danger."

His stomach clenched. "I know, sir. I need to go through everything we have. Look at all the reports from when she worked at the hospital and all the information we have. See if we missed something."

"I agree. Use anyone who's not too busy to help."

Gavin sighed. He would find the truth. "Can you send someone to watch out for Lexie at the clinic, Chief? I won't be able to focus if I'm thinking about her being in danger."

The moment he heard the words spill out of his mouth, Gavin knew that he had just given himself away. He might as well have said "I love her." Chief Paul Kennedy was sharp.

Indeed, even now, the chief was giving him a knowing smile. "Yes, we can do that." Gavin began to leave the room. "Oh, and Gavin…"

He stopped. The chief never called him Gavin. Cautiously, he turned back to the chief. "Yes?" He drew the word out.

The smile widened on the chief's face. "It's not necessarily a bad thing to care for someone. I would even go as far as to say it makes us better people."

There wasn't much he could say to that.

Within minutes he and Parker were poring over all the evidence and interviews. Zee came in to help. They were missing something. Something so obvious, he'd probably kick himself when he found.

Gavin picked up the file containing all the information about the flower shop arson. Opening the file, he started to read through notes. The official report listed the husband and wife owners as deceased. Their bodies had been positively identified. The son's body, however, was too damaged to be identified. He frowned. The report said that the son's body had been covered with accelerant. That was odd. Gavin picked up the family picture and squinted at the grainy image.

All the blood drained from his face. "Parker! Zee! I have something!"

The other officers both dropped the files in their hands and rushed over. They peered over his shoulder. Gavin poked the image of the son with his forefinger. Medium height. Shoulder-length dark hair parted in the middle. Dark eyes. A dimpled smile. All of which he'd seen before.

"This guy here, the son? The police report has him listed as deceased, killed in the fire. The body they had assumed was his? It wasn't. He's not dead."

"Where is he, then?" Zee asked.

"He goes by the name Damien Alexander now. He works at the clinic. As their janitor."

The chief came out at their call. His face went blank. A sure sign that he was concerned. He pointed one finger at Zee. "Find the connection with the hospital. I want this man to be accountable for every murder he committed, and to do that we need proof."

"You." He pointed at Parker. "I want a warrant to search his house, and I want it yesterday."

"Got it, boss." Parker took off.

"Jackson, go find Miss Grant and do whatever you need to in order to protect her."

"On it," Gavin yelled, already heading out the door. He ran to his cruiser, ignoring the icy conditions. Jumping the vehicle, he headed out as fast as could safely be managed. He flipped on the lights and the siren. Cars moved aside as he whipped past them. He was grateful that he didn't have very many traffic lights to deal with on the way to the clinic. He needed every edge he could get.

Lexie was at work today. He'd told Sam they could reopen the clinic. Then he'd walked away from her. And now she was in danger again, and he was miles away. Never in his life had he prayed as hard as he was praying now.

His phone rang. He jabbed the speaker button. "Yeah?"

"Jackson, it's Parker here. I found info on Alexander. He was working at the hospital. Apparently, he'd had aspirations to be a nurse but had a problem with authority. According to his aunt, his father had told him he would no longer pay for schooling if he wasn't going to toe the line. The aunt also said that she'd talked with Damien's father, her brother, and he'd said something about finding that his son had been stealing drugs from the hospital and had decided he needed to own up to his crimes."

"You think the father was planning on turning him in?" Gavin asked.

"I absolutely think that." Parker responded.

"So he torched the place." Gavin tapped his fingers on the steering wheel.

"Yep. That's my take."

Gavin considered the information. "I wonder if the aunt guessed that her nephew hadn't died in the fire."

"If she had," Parker replied, "I think she kept silent for fear he'd come after her next."

"Do we have any idea who might have been the third body found at the flower shop?"

"I asked about that," Parker responded. "At this point, there are no leads."

At the clinic, he braked in front of the building, not caring that his vehicle was taking up two parking spaces.

There were quite a few people hovering around the doorway. As far as he could tell, they were all patients and family members. But there were no doctors or nurses in sight. And no Lexie.

"What's going on here?" he barked at the crowd in general.

One older Amish woman stepped forward.

"We were told to wait outside."

"Why were you told to come out here?"

A younger man spoke up. "There was an emergency inside. Ain't that right, *Dat*?" he asked the bearded man beside him.

The older man coughed before responding. "*Jah*. An emergency."

Several other patients nodded. They all were looking cold and miserable standing out there in the cold.

"Who told you to come out? Was it the doctor? A nurse?"

"Nee," the older woman answered. "It was the man with the broom."

The man with the broom. She had to mean the janitor. Alexander had the whole staff, including his Lexie, trapped inside the building with him. He paced a step away, giving himself room to think. The first thing he needed to do was to get these innocent folks out of harm's way. If bullets started flying or another bomb went off, he didn't want any civilians near the building.

"Folks!" He raised his voice to get their attention. "I need to check out the situation here. I need you all to disperse. Maybe you can wait in the restaurant across the street? Or in the vehicles you came in?"

A couple of the people grumbled, but most moved to do as he said. He heard a couple of people tell their drivers to just take them home. They'd make another appointment. That was fine with him. Fewer people around made his job easier.

Once the sidewalk was cleared, he tried the door. It was locked, as he'd suspected it would be. The blinds were closed, but one was slightly inverted. Bending, he closed one eye and peeked through the opening it made.

The room, or what he could see of it, was empty.

Removing his service weapon, he didn't even take the time to aim. Instead, he used the gun to smash out the window then reached in through the hole and searched with his hand for the lock. When he found it, he unlocked the door and carefully opened it. Shattered glass crunched under his feet.

There was no one in sight. Out of habit, he flipped on his body camera.

Keeping his service weapon pointed in front of him, he walked as quietly as he could across the floor, listening for any sounds. After a few minutes, he breached the hall leading to the examination rooms. He heard voices.

Correction. He heard one voice. A male voice. A voice that he thought he remembered from the initial interview after Noah Hostetler was shot.

Damien Alexander was in the room just beyond him. And he wasn't alone.

"You pushed me to it, Alexa. We belonged together, but you couldn't stay away from the other men. I warned you. You didn't listen. Really, it's your own fault you have to die."

SIXTEEN

Damien Alexander raised his gun toward Alexa. To her shock, Sam stepped in front of her. Apparently, gallantry was bred into both the Jackson men. Their captor shrugged and sneered.

"Don't matter to me which one of youse dies first. None of youse are leaving this room alive."

The door slammed open, hitting him in the arm. The gun discharged once, leaving a hole in the wall. Gavin charged into the room. Damien grabbed Linda, the person closest to him, and held her up against him. He pointed the gun to her temple.

"I'll shoot. You know I will."

Gavin stopped so abruptly, he swayed. His eyes swept over her and the others in the room, checking out their status.

Sam made a move. Was he trying to play the hero?

Damien saw his movement and switched the barrel of the gun to him. He stopped. Gavin's eyes narrowed. No. Oh no.

Damien suddenly threw Linda from him with enough force that her face struck the wall. He didn't even look her way. He had a new target in his sight.

"Since you're so keen to die, Doctor, why don't I just give you what you want?" His finger started to tighten on the trigger.

"No!" Gavin leaped forward, between Sam and Damien. The blast of the gun shocked Alexa. Gavin jerked.

Alexa screamed as Gavin stumbled backward, tripping over his feet. He slammed into the wall, his shoulder catching a shelf, which tilted alarmingly. Then it tipped up, ramming the shelf above it. Both slats of thick wood rushed down. Smacking Gavin on the head. He dropped to the floor and lay there, motionless. Only the slow rise of his chest let her know he was still alive.

"Gavin!" she screamed. But she wasn't the only one. Sam also shouted his brother's name. When he would have moved, Damien turned the gun on Gavin once more.

"I'll shoot him again. And this time, he'll be dead. It's your choice."

Sam halted. Alexa had no doubt that he'd do it, too. *Don't move*, she begged Sam silently. He blanched. His hands fisted, but he stayed where he was. Although he couldn't stop himself from casting anxious glances at his younger brother.

Neither could she.

Damien barked a cold laugh. Sneering, he motioned with the gun toward Sam. "So you can listen to someone other than yourself."

A meaty hand grabbed Alexa's forearm. She shuddered. The urge to struggle swelled up, but she couldn't. He'd shoot Gavin if she gave him the slightest reason.

"Alexa, my dear, we need to leave." He yanked her arm behind her, pushing it high up on her back. Excruciating pain shot through her. He was going to break it if he went too much higher. Tears stung her eyes. She blinked them back; she needed to see.

Still, when he pulled her, she instinctively resisted.

"Don't make me shoot him, Alexa." The malevolent growl in her ear killed any rebellious impulses. "It would give me great pleasure to do so. To destroy the man you betrayed me with."

"Please, no—"

The hand on her arm let go, but only long enough for him to smack her on the side of the head. Ear ringing, she barely noticed when he grabbed the aching arm and again forced it behind her back.

"Don't ever argue with me. We'll go out the back door."

Any thought that someone in the waiting room would see them and intervene died. She knew that no one out there would see them. Megan, the doctor and Marvin's sister were all in the examination room. Which meant no one who worked at the clinic would be coming back to check on things. And if she screamed or made any noise, someone would die.

She was pretty sure that she was going to die. At the moment she couldn't think of any way that she'd be able to avoid that fate. He paused briefly to pull a key out of his pocket and lock the door from the outside. As the janitor, he'd had access to all their systems. And no one at the clinic had even questioned it.

Damien continued to push and pull her out the back door and through the heavy drifts of snow. At one point, he pushed her through a drift that was higher than the tops of her boots. Snow trickled inside. Within minutes her feet were frozen. So was the rest of her, as she had been forced outside without her coat on.

Damien pushed her into a car waiting near the curb. Out in the open. Hope started to build within her. The car had been parked in a handicap space. Maybe someone had spotted it and reported it. If so, there was a chance that people would be looking for the vehicle. Damien started driving, keeping the gun trained on her. It was held low. Other drivers wouldn't be able to see it. However, the patients who had been forced to leave the clinic might become suspicious. She prayed that one of them might decide to call the police. If they did, hopefully her description would soon hit the airwaves. If so, there was a chance someone would recognize her.

Damien threw her a glance. She shuddered at the viciousness she saw in his eyes.

"I thought you were special, Alexa. But you were no better than my parents." His voice was calm, almost conversational. "They were going to betray me, too. I heard my old man talking about it one night. I was smarter than them. Burned their shop down while they were sleeping. The police, they thought all of us were dead."

He gave an ugly chuckle. "There were three bodies, but the one in my room wasn't me. It was the body of a hitchhiker I'd picked up. Just like that, I was a free man. And after I get rid of you, I'll move on again."

Alexa couldn't respond. She'd just about reached her limit.

After a few miles, he pulled over onto a dirt road.

No other vehicles were in sight.

What was he doing? He climbed out of the car and rounded the vehicle to her door, keeping her in his sight all the while. When he yanked her door open, she cringed.

"Get out."

This was it. Well, no one else was around for him to hurt, so she'd take her chances. Scrambling, she made a motion to go for the other door. He grabbed her and pulled her from the car, hurting her as his fingers bit into her arm.

After he dragged her out, he slapped her. Hard. She tasted blood.

He pushed a button on his key fob and the trunk popped open.

Oh no. Suddenly, her fear of small closed-in places was all that she could think of. Struggling with all her might, she fought, trying to kick and scratch, anything to avoid being shoved into the trunk.

Her blows and attempts didn't even faze him. He pulled her irrevocably toward the trunk.

"I can't have anyone recognizing you, Alexa. In you go."

He picked her up and threw her inside, slamming the lid down, closing out all the light.

"Wait! Don't do this!" Ignoring the pain that lanced up the arm he'd held behind her back, Alexa banged on the sealed lid and shouted with all her might. It did no good. She gave up when the car began to vibrate. It was in motion.

Her claustrophobia kicked in, telling her to breathe quickly. She forced herself to remain calm and not panic. Which wasn't easy. Taking in slow breaths, she considered her options. She didn't have her phone on her—it was in her coat. Surely someone from the clinic would have notified the police by now.

Police. Gavin. Was he safe? What would he do?

He'd pray.

Closing her eyes, she tried to think of the right words. Nothing came to mind. Certainly nothing fancy. *God just wants your trust and your love.* Could she do that? Could she trust Gavin's God. Could He help her now?

It was worth a try.

"God, I don't know if I'm doing this right. Please help Gavin. Help me. Amen."

Was that enough?

She tried to keep track of the turns the car made. It was impossible. She also lost any clue as to what time it was. She grew colder. Her teeth knocked together, she was shivering so hard. Her feet were blocks of ice. And then another problem became evident. She could feel her head growing fuzzy. It was hard to focus her thoughts.

Her blood sugar was crashing. The sugar pills she needed were in her bag. So was her glucagon kit. And her bag was back at the clinic. One of her worst fears had always been that she'd go into a diabetic coma and not be able to come out of it. She'd been careful since she'd been diagnosed to have the medicine she needed on hand.

But she had nothing now. No medicine. No food. No doctors. No Gavin. All she had was a maniac who believed that because she'd once treated him, they were soul mates.

Her head was swimming now. Soon she

wouldn't be able to stay alert. Fear crawled through her. Her heart wanted to explode with it. Fear for herself. Fear for Gavin.

And fear for Damien's next victim. Unless he was stopped, the cycle would continue.

"Lord, I have nothing left."

She couldn't even think of the words to say. All she knew was that she was going to die. Gavin found some peace in his relationship with God. She discovered that she wanted that, too. Silently, in the cold dark trunk where she lay, she offered that wish up to God.

Closing her eyes again, a sense of peace washed over her. She had been searching for peace for so long. It had finally come with her surrender to God.

She waited for the end to claim her. "Lord, help Gavin not to blame himself."

A tingling buzz swam in her head, accompanied by the whirling of nausea in her stomach. She was going to pass out. The buzzing increased, swallowing up her last conscious thought.

Poor Gavin. He was going to be too late.

Alexa was gone.

Sam was leaning over him, his face pale and drawn. "Gavin—"

Shoving his brother away, Gavin clambered unsteadily to his feet. Swaying, he fought off the dizziness. His arms were caught on both sides. Too weak to protest, he allowed himself to be assisted to a chair.

After a couple of minutes, the dizziness faded. Opening his eyes, he found himself the focus of the others in the room. Sam. Megan. Linda. But no Lexie, and no Damien.

He had her.

Gavin surged to his feet, nearly knocking Sam over in the process.

"Gavin, you shouldn't—"

"He's got her, Sam! That madman has Lexie. I have to go after her." The sudden vision of that same madman holding a gun on his brother brought him up short. He gave his brother a once-over. He seemed all right. "Are you okay, Sam? You don't look hurt."

"We're all fine. Look, he somehow blocked the door. We can't get out. We've yelled, but no one has come to help us."

"Yeah, that's because when I got here, I made all the patients go away for their own safety."

Sam nodded.

"That was probably for the best. Damien took all of our cell phones when he locked us in here. But he didn't take yours. Megan has used your cell phone to call the police. You were only out for about five minutes. He can't have gone far."

Which was great information. Except that Jackson didn't know how far Alexander was planning on traveling with Lexie. The past few run-ins had led him to believe that he was pretty set on killing her.

Lord, help me think!

"How long ago has it been since you called the police?" He started to pace, refusing to dwell on his aching head. Or his aching heart.

"Three minutes. Maybe four," Megan answered.

Calculating the time and distance in his mind did nothing to improve his mood. Too far away. "It'll still be fifteen minutes before the police arrive," he told them. He could see by the troubled looks on Megan's and Sam's faces that they didn't like that statement any more than he did.

"Oh!" He looked over in surprise at the quiet Amish girl who had exclaimed. Linda. Her eyes were wide. The side of her face was beginning to show the faint purplish hue of a bruise about to form from where Damien had shoved her against the wall. He winced. It had to hurt.

"Yes?"

"If that lady," she said, gesturing toward Megan, "will let me use the phone, I can call my driver. He was only going to go into the hardware store on the next street to wait for me. I usually call him from the office phone, and he comes and gets me. He can come and open the door."

The first glimmer of hope since he'd opened his eyes started to sprout and grow inside his soul. If the driver could come right away, there was a chance he could get to the woman who owned his heart.

Megan leaped to her feet, her face animated. "Yes! Here, call him, please!"

Linda didn't need to be asked twice. Grabbing the phone, she started to enter the digits, saying the phone number to herself. Gavin tapped his heel against the wall while they waited.

"George? *Jah*, it's Linda. Please, George, I need your help." Rapidly, she explained her situation to the man on the other end of the phone. The conversation was less than a minute, but to Gavin, it took forever. Linda ended the call and handed the phone back to Megan.

"He is on his way. The man who owns the hardware store is coming, too."

Within a couple of minutes, the sound of two men working on the door was heard. It took them only a minute or so to get it unjammed. When they opened it, the occupants of the room all burst out, exclaiming and talking over each other. Gavin let them. They could explain what happened all they wanted. He had a killer to catch.

"Gavin! Wait up!"

Aggravated, he spun on his heel to watch Sam hurrying to his side. "What, Sam? I have a job to do."

His brother raised his hands in a conciliatory gesture. "I know you do, little brother. I hope with all my heart you find her, this woman you care for."

Gavin didn't even bother to deny it. His days of keeping his distance were done. He just prayed it wasn't too late. "Thanks, Sam."

He started to turn.

Sam wasn't done. "What can I do? How do I help you to get her back?"

The idea of Sam helping had never occurred to him. Sam had always been the one to sometimes demand help to achieve his goals. A doctor he may be, but he'd never gone out of his way to help anyone but himself. Until now.

People can change, can't they?

Lexie's words struck him. Maybe they could. Maybe his brother could. And so could he.

"Okay," he said, turning to his brother, accepting his offer with sincerity. "I need to find out if anyone saw Damien Alexander and Lexie leave. I have no clue what kind of vehicle he was driving or where he was headed. Any information could help us."

"You got it."

Sam moved across the street to where some people had come out to watch. Gavin headed toward a second group. It took them a few minutes, but by the time Parker arrived, they knew what kind of car Damien was driving and what direction he was heading.

"Parker!" He ran up to his colleague and friend, who was on his radio. "Alexander's driving a dark blue Chevy four-door sedan. They don't know the make of it. One guy did catch the license plate. He said it was the numbers of the year his kid was born." He rattled off the plate number to Parker, who immediately fired them back to the dispatcher.

Starting to back away, Gavin yelled, "I'm heading in the direction they drove."

"I'll follow along. Jace should be here soon."

Knowing that Lieutenant Jace Tucker would be on scene here freed Gavin from any sense of guilt. "Right. I'm out of here."

Parker gave him a thumbs-up.

"Sergeant Jackson!" Gavin spun to see Megan running toward him. She was holding a small zippered bag in her hand. "You might need this. It's Alexa's diabetes kit."

"Thanks!" Grabbing the bag, Gavin headed for his vehicle.

Jumping into his cruiser, Gavin tossed the bag on the passenger seat. Then he jammed the key into the ignition and turned. The car roared to life. Jerking it into reverse, he pulled out of his parking space, then moved off in pursuit of the woman he loved.

I'm coming, Lexie. I'm coming. Please just hold on.

SEVENTEEN

The cruiser slid into a turn. The wheels spun on the gravel, spitting out dirt and stones. Gavin could hear the gravel chunks pelting the underside of the vehicle. He removed his foot from the gas long enough for the car to settle before he again sped up.

His siren was blaring out a warning for other vehicles to get out of his way, the blue and red lights flashing like a disco strobe light. Traffic moved aside for him. Glancing in his back mirror, he could see another cruiser following close behind. Parker. Good.

Lord, let us catch Alexander before he hurts Lexie.

"The suspect has been spotted heading west on Marrell Avenue," Elise's clear voice cut across the air.

"Yes!" He would be at Marrell in two minutes. And Marrell was one of those roads with very few roads to turn onto. Long stretches with only fields on both sides. He hazarded a glance at his GPS. A plan formulated in his mind. It could work if he turned at the next intersection. Jabbing his finger at the radio on his dashboard, he shouted, "Parker! I'm going to turn on the next road and head north. I'm going to try to cut him off. If you stay on Marrell, we can box him in."

"Got it," Parker responded.

Breaking the connection, Gavin crossed his hands and spun the steering wheel, swerving the cruiser to the left in the intersection. The road was narrow, and he had to slow down to take it safely. Even as frustration tightened his hands on the wheel, he tamped it down. It would do Lexie no good if he crashed. He needed to be safe just as much as he needed to be fast.

A soft litany of prayer streamed forth from his mouth as he continued to drive.

Twenty minutes later, the road he was on ran parallel with Marrell. Glancing to the right, he saw the blue of Alexander's vehicle about a car length ahead of him. Not for long. He grinned, clenching his teeth. His knuckles tightened on the steering wheel and his foot pressed down on the gas pedal. The engine revved. It was a beautiful sound. Alexander's car was an old beater. It gave off a lot of exhaust, but it had no real punch to it. His cruiser, though, now it was a machine. Already, he was gaining on Alexander.

The exhilaration he felt was short-lived. A single glance over at the car he was racing parallel to made his blood freeze in his veins.

Lexie wasn't in the car.

At least, he couldn't see her. He forced himself to remain calm, to keep his wits about him. There were a multitude of possible reasons why he couldn't see her. Maybe Alexander was making her stay down in the back seat. Maybe she was sitting in the floorboard.

Maybe she was dead.

No, no, no! He would not give in to those thoughts. It wasn't going to be like last time. He wasn't going to lose someone else he loved because he wasn't on time. He would see her again. And when he did, he would tell her how he felt and do his best to convince her to give him a chance. Even if he didn't deserve it.

But first he had a killer to catch.

The bend was just ahead. As soon as he rounded the curve, the two roads would merge into one and run concurrently for the next five miles. Now was his chance. Setting his jaw,

Gavin jammed his foot on the gas as far as it would go. His cruiser roared and shot forward, skimming the curve like a skater rounding the arena. He pulled on the steering wheel, veering his vehicle so that it was perpendicular across the road, blocking it. Parker's cruiser was advancing rapidly from behind.

Whipping his head up, his steady gaze met Alexander's panicked eyes. He could see the other man frantically turning his wheel, but he had nowhere to go. There were trees on one side, a guardrail on the other. And in front, the steel frame of Gavin's car. Still, he didn't give up. His car slammed into the guardrail with a sickening crunch. Gavin flinched, praying that Lexie hadn't been injured in the crash.

Throwing the door open, Damien Alexander leaped from the car and bolted toward the trees. A tactical error. Gavin jumped from his own vehicle and ran him down. Alexander was hampered by a limp. There was a bloody gash in his jeans. He'd obviously been hurt when the car had crashed into the guardrail.

With a single leap, Gavin took him down. They landed together on the packed snow. The man was shouting insensibly as Gavin rolled him on his back and slapped handcuffs on his wrists, reciting the Miranda rights quicker than he'd ever done before. All the while, his heart and mind were focused on finding Lexie. Saving Lexie.

Parker arrived at his side as he finished. The two officers hefted the belligerent criminal to his feet. He still wouldn't give up, kicking and fighting the whole way.

Gripping Alexander tightly by the shoulder and arm, Gavin spoke through clenched teeth. "Where is she?"

A smirk crossed Alexander's face. "I told her she'd pay for betraying me. I told her. You think she's yours?" He spat in Gavin's face. "She's mine. She loves me. Or she did. Now she won't be able to betray me ever again."

For a moment black spots danced before Gavin's eyes. He was too late. This evil man had killed her. He'd never see her again. Grief like he'd never known swirled inside him.

He's lying. The thought was a desperate one, but he clung to it like a man dying of thirst. He couldn't give up now, not when he was this close.

"Parker," he barked at his friend. "Take him and put him in the cruiser, will you? I need to search for Lexie. Something tells me this dude is lying."

"You got it." Parker grabbed Alexander

from behind, one hand firmly holding on to his wriggling shoulder, and pushed him toward his vehicle. The lights were still flashing. "You're going away for a long time."

Alexander struggled harder. "No! No, you can't have her! She's mine. She belongs to me!"

Gavin listened to the shrieks, and some of his fear bled away. The man wouldn't carry on so if she was truly dead.

He took a moment to glance inside the vehicle. Lexie wasn't inside the car. If she was still in the vehicle at all, she had to be in the trunk. Reaching inside the car, he pushed the button to release the trunk and then raced to the back of the car.

His heart stopped.

Lexie was lying, so still and pale. All his fears returned. Then he saw she was breathing.

Her diabetes kit! Remembering the bag in his car, he ran back and yanked it out of the front seat. Rummaging through it, he found what he had been looking for—Alexa's glucagon kit. Grabbing it, he quickly returned to her. Then he bent over and lifted her out of the trunk. Her head lolled against his shoulder. "Come on, Lexie. Fight. Don't give in. Lexie, please, open your eyes. Let me see your eyes."

No response.

"Parker! Call 911!" He couldn't take his eyes off her beautiful face. She was so pale. The bruises on her cheeks stood out starkly.

"Done." Parker appeared beside them. "Do you have anything you can give her?"

"Yeah. Help me."

Between the two men, they managed to roll her into the proper position for Gavin to give her the glucagon shot.

A moan caught their attention. Both men's eyes shot to her face. Her lids fluttered open. Her gaze was unfocused and confused, the pupils huge in her blue-gray eyes. They were the most beautiful thing he'd ever seen.

"Gavin?" His name was a mere mumble on her lips, but he understood it. Her mouth moved. She was trying to talk again but couldn't seem to get the words out. He put his finger on her lips to still them. It couldn't be good for her to use so much effort when she was in such bad shape.

"Right here, Lexie. I got you. You're going to be fine. The ambulance is on its way."

"He shot you."

He'd almost forgotten that in his concern about her. "It's just a minor wound. Seriously. I'm good."

"Glad." She fell back asleep in his arms.

He kissed her forehead, thanking God for getting him there in time. Her skin was so cold. She needed to be warmed up, soon. The ambulance arrived, and he released her into the paramedics' care, knowing they could help her in ways he couldn't. Not that it was easy. The only thing he wanted was to go with her.

But he had a job to finish. He needed to see that Alexander was put behind bars and the people at the clinic gave their statements so that the killer would stay in prison for a long, long time. Then Gavin would be able to go to ask for Lexie's pardon and finally work on putting them on the right path to a future together.

The first voice she heard was the intercom calling for Dr. Spencer. Alexa wrinkled her forehead. Her head throbbed where Damien had struck her. Then he'd shoved her into the trunk. The memory of the dank, closed-in space overwhelmed her for a moment before she was able to shrug it off. She wasn't in the car anymore, thankfully. Gingerly, she opened her eyes. Then slammed them shut again as the glare from the fluorescent light hit them. She was in the hospital.

Alexa squished her eyelids together as she fought to keep back the memories of everything that had occurred since Damien Alexander had forced her from the clinic. A shudder ripped through her, hard. Even her teeth chattered.

The vision of Gavin falling, blood dripping on the white tiles, swallowed her up. *He's okay,* she reminded herself. *He came to save you.*

Or did she dream that? No. She couldn't have. The memory of him jabbing the glucagon injection into her leg was too clear. As was his voice, deep and rugged with pain, telling her to fight. Not to give in.

And she hadn't. His voice had been her anchor. She'd followed it back from the dark place she'd been in and struggled to keep her eyes open. To keep his beloved face in her sight. She'd tried to get her mouth to move to tell him she loved him. Her swollen tongue wouldn't obey. She wouldn't let the next opportunity pass her by.

If there was one. Would he come to see her? After all they'd been through, she couldn't—wouldn't—believe that she was only a case to be solved to him. She'd heard the emotion in his voice, felt the care in his touch. That had to mean something. It had to.

And what about Damien Alexander? She shivered as she considered the man who'd stalked her and been responsible for so much death and grief. What about Sam? And the others? She recalled the way that Gavin had thrown himself in front of the gun, taking the bullet for his brother. Even as she flinched remembering, warmth blossomed in her chest. As hurt and betrayed as he had felt by what had happened in the past, he still risked his life for his brother. Maybe there was hope there.

Maybe she should hand the whole situation over to God.

God can heal them. Yes, God could. *Please, Lord. Help Gavin repair his relationship with his family.* Every prayer came easier. God had already proved that He was on her side. Even when she was near death, He had let her know that He was there and that she was loved. The peace that had filled her was unlike anything she'd ever experienced before.

But she hadn't died. She was alive. Taking a deep breath in through her nose, she held it in her lungs for a moment before letting it out. After being in the trunk, taking a deep breath was a luxurious sensation.

She felt almost human again. Well, except for the IV in her arm. And the monitors surrounding her. Anything was better than the alternative. For a brief moment, she was back in the trunk of the car. The memory of the closed-in space and the light-headed sensation as her blood sugar bottomed out caused her to shudder.

"I nearly died today," she said aloud, shivering at the stark words. "Thank You, Lord. Thank You for protecting me. Thank You for bringing Gavin to me."

"It's my fault he took you." Gavin's voice reached out to her from the doorway. She jerked her head toward the door. The anguish in his voice was mirrored on his face. None of his normal confidence was in evidence. Instead, the pain she saw blatantly displayed seared straight through her to her heart. "Because of my stubbornness, I could have lost you."

Unable to bear his agony, she reached out her hand, the one unencumbered by the IV. He slowly moved into the room. She was afraid he wouldn't take her hand. He did. She sighed. Then winced. His grip was tight. But she wouldn't complain. He was here, and he needed her.

"Gavin, you're not to blame. How could you even think that?" He was still too far away. Patting the bed next to her, she urged him to sit. He hesitated. Then gently, he settled himself on the edge.

Reaching out a hand, he brushed her hair off her forehead. His warm fingers lingered on her cheek. She turned her head slightly into his hand. All too soon, his arm dropped.

"Lexie, my uncle died because I missed his phone call. Today, I thought it was going to happen again. I thought you were going to die because I wasn't there for you."

"Hush. You can't always control what happens, Gavin." How could she get through to him? "When I was stuffed in that trunk," she began, ignoring his wince, "I realized something. I knew that no matter what happened to me, I was in God's hands. I wasn't alone. He was with me. Gavin, I can't explain it, but at that moment, all I could do was trust. I know it sounds weird, but it was a huge moment of grace for me."

He lifted his eyes to hers. "I'm glad. So you don't blame me?"

"I don't blame you. I blame Damien Alexander. He's the one responsible for everything that happened."

"Yeah. Before I forget, your brother and his family are on their way. I found your cell phone in Damien's possession. I hope you don't mind, but I looked up Allen's number in your contacts. I had to call him. He was very concerned. He really loves you, you know?"

Tears filled her eyes. She blinked them back, nodding. "I know that now."

Gavin scratched his head.

"So." He drew out the word, suddenly awkward. "I was wondering, that is, I was hoping that maybe now that you're safe, we could go out on a real date. You know, like a normal couple."

A smile stretched her lips. If it looked the way she felt, it was probably a goofy one. She didn't care. "I know exactly what I want to do. I want to go get a Christmas tree. I want to celebrate. Will you help me pick it out?"

That casual grin she loved so much flashed across his face. "Absolutely! We can decorate it together. The first Christmas of many together." His face darkened with doubt. "Unless you don't care for me that way."

Oh, that man! That strong, sweet stubborn man! After all they'd been through, he still wasn't sure of her feelings for him. It didn't matter. She loved him. And she needed to tell him. Sucking in a deep breath, she braced herself for his reaction.

"Of course I care for you. Gavin Jackson, whether you feel the same or not, I love you."

She let the words hang in the air between them, waiting.

At first he didn't react. She felt a little panicky. Then, a slow grin bloomed across his face. That familiar, confident smile that took her breath away.

"Yeah?" he said, his voice smooth, reaching out and capturing her hand in his.

A wave of emotion swirled over her. She had to swallow to speak around it. "Yeah," she responded.

"Well, I'm glad to know that, Alexa Grant. 'Cause I'm in love with you. Completely."

She could do nothing about the smile that spread across her face.

The door swung open suddenly. A nurse bustled in, concern etched on her face. Her face smoothed out, and a knowing smirk took its place as she saw Gavin and Lexie sitting together.

"Your heart rate sped up, honey. Are you feeling all right?" The twinkle in her eyes suggested she already knew the answer.

"I'm fine, Zoe."

The nurse grinned at her and strolled back toward the door. As she opened it, however, she paused and tossed Alexa a wink over her shoulder. Had Gavin seen that? Cutting her eyes to him, she saw the wide smile pasted on his handsome face. Oh, yeah, he'd seen it.

"Bye, Zoe," Alexa said pointedly. Zoe stepped out and closed the door. Her laughter drifted back into the room.

Alexa was too happy to be embarrassed. The bed shook. A glance over at Gavin explained why. He was laughing silently, his shoulders jerking.

"Hey, you shouldn't laugh." She pointed at him accusingly. She didn't mean it, though. Happiness bubbled up inside her and gurgled out in a trickling laugh.

"Lexie," Gavin murmured, moving closer. "I love the sound of your laugh. I hope to hear it every day from now on."

Her breath caught in her throat at the warm look he bestowed on her.

"Oh?" Was that husky voice hers? She cleared her throat. Her heart was thudding wildly in her chest. "I'm good with that." He leaned in closer. His warm scent teased her nostrils. "We should seal this agreement properly," he said.

"How do we do that?" she breathed.

"Like this."

He closed the remaining distance between them and kissed her gently.

Alexa allowed her eyelids to drift shut. She kissed him back. It was kiss of tenderness and healing. A kiss that said she was cherished, she was worthy.

She was loved.

EPILOGUE

"Isn't it time yet?" Gavin glanced at the clock on the wall for the fifth time—11:40. Four minutes later than the last time he'd checked.

"Jackson, relax. It's almost time." He could hear the eye roll in Parker's amused voice.

Parker was standing near the window he'd just opened to let the slight breeze in. Gavin could smell the roses that bloomed directly outside the window. Parker's gold band, which had been there since his own wedding in April, glinted in the sunlight. One more blessing. After five days of solid rain, the August day had dawned clear and sunny.

"Sure, it's fine for you to laugh. You've already done this." Gavin narrowed his eyes at Parker, but he wasn't really annoyed. His friend's presence helped keep him from totally going insane as the time until the beginning of the wedding ceremony continued to drag on.

Parker laughed. He made no bones about the fact that he was a happily married man. Gavin could hardly believe how anxious he was to be married. Married to Lexie.

Gavin had always prided himself on being calm and steady. Not today. Today he was so nervous that he'd dropped the small square velvet-covered box twice. Which made him even more nervous. He could only imagine meeting Alexa in front of the church and explaining to her that he didn't have her wedding band because he'd lost it.

Her wedding band. Awe filled him. He was getting married today. He glanced at the clock again. Married in ten minutes. After resigning himself to a solitary life, God had moved in and changed his life. Changed his heart.

"Easy, bro. You want me to hold that box for you?" Sam placed his hand on his brother's shoulder.

Another wonder. Gavin hadn't thought he and Sam would ever be able to move past what had happened. Seeing a gun pointing at his brother, though, had opened his eyes to what was really important. It had taken time, but in the past eight months, Sam and Gavin had made great strides in healing their relationship.

Enough so that Gavin had asked his brother to be his best man.

"Guys, let's get this show on the road," Parker said, slapping his hands together and rubbing them. Gavin couldn't agree more.

After today, he'd no longer be alone. No more solitary life.

Gavin allowed a small smile to escape as he appreciated God's sense of humor. He'd planned on being an island, yet in spite of himself, he'd forged strong friendships with a group of exceptional men and women. No longer did he want to be alone.

Excitement zinged inside him, building until he felt like he would burst from it.

"I'm ready. Let's do this."

The men filed out of the room. Within minutes they were standing at the front of the church. Gavin's throat grew tight as he watched Sergeant Miles Olsen escort his mother to her seat, his father following behind them. His mom looked lovely in a silver and lavender dress. From where he stood, he could see that her smile was tremulous. He rolled his eyes, his heart filled with affection. She was already crying.

As he looked over the church, he could see his other friends and colleagues in the pews.

Jace Tucker sat with his wife and daughter, and next to him was Chief Kennedy and his family. The boys looked like little men in their suits. Irene was holding their new baby girl, Anya, against her shoulder. Despite the doctor's concerns, her baby had been just fine. Her name was actually Antonia, but Irene's younger son, Matthew, didn't like that name and shortened it.

Irene's boys been thrilled to be adopted by Paul. AJ, the older boy, asked Paul if that meant they could call him Dad. Gavin remembered how an uncharacteristically emotional chief had relayed the conversation. Apparently, AJ and Matthew had decided that it would be okay to call their stepdad Dad since their real father would always be Daddy. In that way, they were able to keep both men separate and special.

Miles moved to take his seat next to his wife, Rebecca, who was holding their three-month-old son. Elise Parker sat near them, holding Elise's squirming nephew, Mikey, whom she was raising. He grinned at the child's antics. That little boy was a bundle of energy. He was a joy to watch. Gavin knew that Parker was in the process of adopting the child.

Dan Willis was there with his family, too.

The twins, Rory and Siobhan, were almost six. They sat still between Dan and his wife, Maggie, but Gavin could see that mischief was alight in their eyes. Their two-year-old son, Jack, was asleep on Dan's shoulder.

His eyes slid over to where Lacey sat behind his parents. When he'd first seen her at Christmas, it had felt awkward at first. But he was glad to note that his bitterness toward her was gone. In fact, he felt nothing more than relief. That's when he realized that his parents had been right. She had never been the right choice for him. She was a good wife for Sam, though.

His musings were interrupted by the beginning of the wedding march. His heart started pounding. This was it. His nervousness fled. In its place was anticipation. He barely saw the bridesmaids as Megan and Claire walked down the aisle. His eyes were searching the back of the church for the first glimpse of his bride.

Suddenly, she was there.

His breath got stuck in his throat. She was the loveliest woman he had ever seen. Her blond hair was upswept. It wasn't her dress or her hair that held his attention, though. It was the joyful smile on her face, a smile that was just for him. It beamed out her joy and love as clearly as if she'd shouted it to him.

He focused on Lexie as she walked down the aisle on the arm of her brother, Allen.

Thank You, Lord. Help me be worthy of this woman You've blessed me with.

Lexie reached his side and placed her hand in his.

An hour later, they left the church, husband and wife.

Laughing, Lexie and Gavin held hands as they ducked and ran the gauntlet of well-wishers that lined up outside the church doors. The guests blew bubbles at the newlyweds as they dashed down the path and out to the limousine that was waiting to bring them to the reception hall. The uniformed driver held the door opened for them. Once inside the vehicle, they both sighed. The silence enveloped them softly.

Looking into Lexie's eyes, Gavin felt like he'd just returned home after a long journey.

"I love you," he whispered. It was no longer hard to say.

Her eyes softened. "I love you, too, Gavin."

They leaned toward each other, meeting in the middle for a gentle kiss. His stubborn pride had almost cost him his brother. And more than that. He'd almost given up on finding a love of his own. He would have missed out on the devotion and care of this sweet woman.

Thank You, Jesus.

Lexie sighed and rested her head against his shoulder. The sweet, fresh scent of her hair tickled his nose. Inhaling, he smiled and kissed his bride on the top of her head.

He couldn't wait to find out what the future held for them.

* * * * *

If you enjoyed this book, don't miss the other heart-stopping Amish adventures from Dana R. Lynn's Amish Country Justice series:

Plain Target
Plain Retribution
Amish Christmas Abduction
Amish Country Ambush

Find more great reads at www.LoveInspired.com.

Dear Reader,

Another author once told me that her own personal experiences somehow found their way onto the pages as she wrote. After writing my seventh Love Inspired Suspense, I believe it. A piece of me is in each book, including this one.

I'd started writing the story when my family was faced with the challenge of diabetes. I had much to learn! I decided to have Alexa share this challenge. The hero needed to understand it, too.

Gavin Jackson is charismatic, with a chip on his shoulder and a stubborn streak. He is also a man who takes caring for others to heart. He had lost much in the past, but Alexa is just the right woman to convince him to risk his heart again.

I love to hear from readers! To connect, you may visit me on my website, www.danarlynn. com or find me on Facebook and Twitter.

Blessings,
Dana R. Lynn

HOME on the RANCH